GROUPER
MOON

GROUPER MOON

WRITTEN AND ILLUSTRATED BY
CYNTHIA SHAW

AURELIA PRESS

To my husband and sons, Tim, Pat, John and David; and my parents, Bill and Averil Cooper. Yes, Mom, it's done.

I wish to thank the following for their help, encouragement, and constructive reviews: Tom and Liz Cooper, Andrew Dye, Benjamin Dye, Marlene Hill Donnelly, Dr. Anne-Marie Eklund, Peggy Estes, Simon Hackshaw, Joan Lee, Jaynie Martz, Rachel Mehrtens, Rebecca Moeckel, Michael Saha, Neena Saha, Dr. Barbara Temple-Thurston, Pat Turpin, Stan Waterman, and Merrianne West.

For their help and generosity with scientific expertise: Phillippe Bush, Department of the Environment, Cayman Islands; Anne-Marie Eklund, Ph.D., Research Fishery Biologist, NOAA-Fisheries; and Jill Grover, Ph.D., Hatfield Marine Science Center and Caribbean Marine Research Center.

Special thanks to my editor, Dr. Susan Sullivan.

While the science and issues in GROUPER MOON are real, the story, setting and characters are fictitious, and intended to bear no resemblance to anyone except, occasionally, myself.

GROUPER MOON
Written and Illustrated by Cynthia Shaw
Photography by Cynthia Shaw
Photo reference for "Time to Boogey" provided by Stan Waterman

Published by Aurelia Press
P. O. Box 1426
Richland, WA 99352
Phone (509) 627-0751
www.aureliapress.com

Library of Congress Catalog Number: 99-90928
ISBN 0-9670595-2-6
First Edition
Printed in the USA

[1. Grouper fisheries—Fiction. 2. Conservation of natural resources—Fiction [1. Fishery conservation. 2. Coral reef conservation.] 3. Coral reef ecology—Fiction. 4. Economic development, Environmental aspects—Fiction 5. Economic development, Sociological aspects—Fiction. 6. Ecotourism—Fiction.]

CONTENTS

FOREWORD

by Stan Waterman
Producer, Films Under the Sea

It is a too-rare treat for me to encounter an author who, with complete success, can provide accurate science within an appealing story. The author of GROUPER MOON is a veteran diver. She has the perceptive eye of a scientist for marine animal behavior. By happy circumstance she also has a magic touch in gracefully anthropomorphizing the substance of her story so that it has both appeal and perspective for the young reader.

The schooling of groupers in parts of the Caribbean is a mating phenomenon that few divers have been fortunate enough to witness. I happen to be one who has, and I have also witnessed the unrestricted catch by native fishermen from Belize during the mass mating syndrome. The author smoothly addresses the obvious disaster threatening the grouper population and explains, with a broader view, the disasters that lie ahead—and indeed, presently exist—in over-harvesting our natural resources in the sea.

The grouper romance is charming. Teenage readers will find it appealing. It is saved from the sappy, sugary dimension so often achieved by authors who imbue their animal characters with human personalities. E. B. White and Kenneth Grahame had the style that gave their animal characters believable voice and thought. Cynthia Shaw has it, too.

I read the story of GROUPER MOON with great pleasure. I also learned that there is much a marine scientist sees in grouper behavior that I have missed in my fifty-odd years of diving with them.

GROUPER

MOON

CHAPTER I

The Gift

I T was Christmas on the Caribbean island of Macquerupa. Renny slipped through the mosquito netting and jumped from his bed. Pulling on his shorts, he peeked around his bedroom door into the tiny living room. Sunlight streamed in through the wooden shutters, setting the yellow room aglow. The chatter of jungle birds drifted in through the screens on the light breeze of early morning. The air smelled fresh.

A potted palm branch stood in the corner of the living room. Draped with colorful paper chains and silver foil birds, it sparkled in the sunlight. Under it lay a small, flat, oblong package wrapped in red paper. Renny tiptoed over. A tag with his name was tied to the white bow. Renny started to reach for the present, but stopped himself.

I'll jinx it if I do that, he thought. He wanted to stretch out the suspense as long as he could. After all, gifts came his way only twice a year—on his birthday and on Christmas.

But I'll bet it'll be somethin' big, 'cause they're always tellin' me that big things come in little packages, Renny thought. He was often teased for being shorter than other kids his age. His parents were fond of reminding him that he had great potential, regardless of his size.

Renny heard his mom and dad stirring in their room. Hurrying back to his own room, he pulled a blue tee shirt out of his drawer and threw it on over his head. Grabbing two small, neatly wrapped presents and a potted hibiscus plant from his dresser top, he scurried back to the living room. He slipped the gifts for his parents under the palm branch. Then he slid into a chair, grabbed a magazine, and pretended to read, as if there was nothing unusual about the day.

Mrs. Thomas was still groggy as she stumbled to the kitchen in her coral-pink robe to put on the coffee. She was a short, plump woman with medium-brown skin. Her curly black hair was wrapped in a turquoise kerchief.

Mr. Thomas grunted and rubbed the back of his neck as he limped behind his wife on cramped feet. He was headed straight for the front porch, where he could wake up and watch the sea birds while he drank his coffee and read the newspaper. He loved his view from the mountainside overlooking Cocoa Bay.

Renny watched as his parents bumbled through their morning rituals. Neither seemed to notice their son. Renny was used to their waking-up routine, but he wasn't sure how long much longer he could wait for them to get through it. The normally patient boy squirmed and scratched his left arm. He rubbed his nose, then his cheek.

"Where *is* the paper!" Mr. Thomas suddenly thundered from the porch. His deep, exuberant voice carried well through the house.

Dishes rattled from the kitchen. "I don't know where the paper *is*," Renny's mom barked back, wiping up spilled water from the countertop.

"Well, I can't start my day without the news!" Mr. Thomas bellowed.

Renny could stand it no longer and blurted, "Hey Mom! Hey Dad! Don't you guys even remember what day it is?"

There was no reply. Then both parents appeared in the living room. They looked at each other, seeming confused. They looked at Renny. Then they looked at the decorated palm branch, and shook their heads.

"Oh," said Mrs. Thomas, pretending surprise. "Maybe that is why there *is* no paper." She stifled a giggle.

"Hmmph. So it is," said Mr. Thomas, winking to his wife.

The aroma of fresh coffee filled the room, and the adults began to perk up a bit. Soon fortified with mugs of the strong beverage, they sat down in their favorite chairs. The chair frames were made of bent bamboo, and had overstuffed cushions with bright green lizards printed on a white, nubby background.

"Well then, merry Christmas," said Mrs. Thomas. She got up to kiss and ruffle the top of her son's head, and then sat back down again.

Taking his cue, Renny jumped up to distribute his gifts to his parents. With great flourish, he placed the hibiscus plant in front of his mother.

"Ooooh. It is my favorite color, coral-pink!" she squealed.

"I grew it myself from a cuttin' from Auntie's yard," replied Renny, adding quickly, "She said I could."

"New fish hooks! I needed these," said Mr. Thomas. He was a fisherman.

"Ooooh, and a new apron! It is my *other* favorite color, sea-green," beamed Mrs. Thomas. "How did you know what I needed?" She was a cook, and ran a tiny cafe called "Margaret's Kitchen."

"I made it in school. The teacher made all of us make 'em," blushed Renny.

"Well, it's very nicely done, dear," said Mrs. Thomas, inspecting his work.

"Hmmm…" said Mr. Thomas, casually rubbing the stubble on his chin. "Say, did old Santy Claws come yet, Renny?"

Finally! Renny thought the moment would never come. "I think he left me somethin' big in that little package under the tree," he said eagerly.

"Well, then go ahead, open it up—hurry, quickly!" his father urged, with a wave of his hand.

And so with excitement that comes only on Christmas, Renny tore into the small package. But his face—along with the wrapping—fell to the floor as he pulled out the contents.

"Huh?" muttered Renny in disbelief. He held up a pair of socks, one in each hand. They were black, and thick.

Renny avoided his parents' eyes as he forced a smile and said, "Thanks. Hey, these uh, socks are pretty cool. Jus' what I always wanted." His cheeks and ear tips burned. Renny looked at the Christmas tree and sighed. His shoulders sagged.

But Renny didn't see the twinkling of his parents' eyes as they casually put their hands over their mouths to conceal smiles.

"Oh, *my*," said Mr. Thomas after a long pause, clearing his throat. He uncrossed his legs, put down his coffee, and leaned forward in his chair. Folding his hands between his knees, he looked up at his wife. "Margaret, dear, I think we might've missed somethin'. Isn't there somethin' over by the door? What is that over there by the door, dear?"

Everyone looked toward the door that led to the front porch. Leaning against the wall was a brown burlap gunnysack wrapped around something long and about a foot wide. It was tied at the top with a green ribbon.

"Oh, but I have no idea. Where did it come from?" said Mrs. Thomas. Turning to Renny, she added, "Why don't you go on over to the door and see what that is?"

Renny hesitated. He was starting to catch on to something fishy. Slowly, he got up and walked across the room. He stopped at the door and looked at the sack. Stooping down, the boy tentatively patted the contours of the sack with his hands. He paused, and patted the sack again. Could it really *be*—? He wanted to savor the moment, just in case it was.

Finally, he pulled off the ribbon and opened the gunny-sack. Then he peered inside.

Renny's eyebrows shot up. It *was!* He couldn't believe his eyes as he pushed down the burlap.

"Oh, wow," Renny said softly. His eyes shone as he put the fins on his feet. Only in his very wildest dreams had he ever worn—or even touched—skin diving fins that were this long. It didn't matter that they were already scuffed up from use. Renny stood up, shook his feet, one at a time, and wiggled his toes.

"They are kind of loose," he said, quickly adding, "but I'm growin' faster now."

"That's what the socks are for," said Mrs. Thomas. "They're extra thick so you can wear them inside the fins until your feet catch up."

Renny jumped up to hug his parents and immediately tripped forward over the fins.

"But you have to take them off when you're in the house," his dad said with a straight face. Everyone laughed.

Renny pulled off the fins, and got back up. This time, his smile was not forced.

"Wow. Thanks. These *are* jus' what I wanted!"

"They were J.D.'s. Said he had 'em when he was about your age. He thought you'd like 'em. He says they're real good fins—and that they'll make you go fast! He said he'd trade 'em for one of your mama's famous dinners, even though I really think he's hopin' you'll give him a hand down at the dive shop. But dinner he'll get, and lobster and grouper are his very favorites, he says. So why don't you go on out after church today and see if you can catch any, 'cause he's comin' tonight," Mr. Thomas said.

"But we are havin' roast pork today," protested Mrs. Thomas. Pork was the traditional island Christmas dinner.

"So we'll have pork and seafood both," answered her husband. "What's wrong with that?"

"Can I skip church today?" asked Renny. He was eager to get in the water with his new fins.

His parents turned and glared at him.

"Jus' thought I'd ask," said Renny, grinning.

"Well, you can stop your grinnin' like a monkey and get ready to go now," said his mother.

All during church, Renny couldn't stop thinking about his new fins. He was giddy with excitement, and couldn't believe they were his. With such long fins, he could be faster and more powerful in the water than ever before. He imagined himself gliding over the reef, diving to new depths. Now the patch reefs would be within easy reach—maybe even the drop-off...

Nah, he'd better not even think about that. The drop-off was forbidden. But so what, he thought. A whole new world was opened up, and he was eager to explore it. Renny's hand sailed through the air in a smooth, sharklike motion as he imagined himself underwater. He was humming.

A jab of his mother's elbow to his ribs brought him back to the present. Renny straightened up, and remembered to thank the Baby Jesus for having J.D. give him his fins.

CHAPTER II

Coconut Cove

I'M goin' out to the reef now," announced Renny, heading for the back porch. The screen door slammed as Renny took his speargun from a hook on the wall. He gave the rubber sling a few tugs, and grabbed his snorkeling gear.

"Stay away from the drop-off, you hear? And quit slammin' the door!" his mother answered from the kitchen. With no glass in the windows, there was a lot of yelling between the inside and outside of the house.

"Yes ma'am!" Renny called back from the yard, picking up speed. He had heard the warning many times. There were sharks out there, and swift currents that would carry him off to where he would never be seen again. Renny hoisted his long fins over his shoulder and started running across the grass toward a shortcut through the jungle. The fins flapped against the backs of his legs.

"Careful with that speargun!" yelled his father from his perch on the porch.

"Yessir!" Renny slowed back down to a fast walk. He'd heard that warning many times, too. He disappeared through a clump of banana trees into the steamy jungle. The air was heavy with the familiar odor of rotting leaves.

"It is the smell of productivity!" his aunt, Opal Brown, had often remarked. "Everythin' growin', dyin', and goin' back to the ground to rot and feed new life. In the jungle, it all happens very fast, over an' over again." Auntie Opal knew just about everything there was to know about anything.

Renny emerged from the jungle onto the road and ran toward Coconut Cove. His bare feet danced on the sizzling asphalt pavement and leapt over puddles and potholes. A sudden shower had come up earlier and emptied the sky of rain. Just as quickly, the clouds had parted and the sun had returned. The rainy season was just ending, and soon road improvements would begin. Men with cutlasses and chain saws had already started to clear the jungle back from the roadsides, exposing the road to the hot midday sun.

Rain had washed orange dirt from some of the cleared areas onto the road. Renny stopped briefly to rinse off his muddy feet in a puddle. His speargun and new fins were getting heavy.

The road emptied into an old parking lot surrounded by mango, coconut and pawpaw (papaya) trees. Renny skipped over weeds that crowded through long, jagged cracks in the crumbling pavement. Nearby were remains of tennis courts, surrounded by a rusty chain-link fence that sagged and was full of holes. In the corner of the parking lot, a set of concrete steps led up to a pile of concrete rubble overgrown with jungle vines. Near the rubble stood an enormous flamboyant. The sprawling tree marked the top of a long, straight set of concrete steps that led down to the beach. Renny stopped to pick up one of its long, brown seed pods from the ground. "Cha cha—cha cha cha!" he chanted softly, rattling the seed pod and wiggling his hips to the rhythm.

Renny reached the steps and hopped on the steel railing, slick from years of kids' bottoms sliding down it. Renny loved the feel of bamboo leaves brushing lightly against him as he floated down. When the railing flattened at a landing, he jumped off and continued lightly down the steps, tossing the rattler aside. Once on the beach, he sat down on a fat piece of driftwood under an almond tree. Renny dug his feet into the cool, moist sand. A thin veil of water washed up over them.

The beach smelled of barnacles and seaweed. It was empty and quiet, except for waves washing up gently on the beach.

A sudden outburst of squawking and heavy wing-flapping from above startled Renny. His eye caught flashes of red and yellow as several rowdy parrots swooped from branch to branch in the jungle on the mountainside.

"You 'ole rogues!" he shouted. They were as obnoxious as they were beautiful. He loved them.

Renny unrolled his catch bag and retrieved his

new socks. After rinsing sand off his feet, he put on the new socks. They were tight. Good, he thought. They won't slip around and give me blisters.

To Renny's right were the ladder-shaped remains of a concrete foundation that had supported a row of tiny changing rooms. To his left was an old concrete platform that had been the floor of a snack bar some thirty years before. The small beach and property at the top of the steps had once been an officers' club belonging to an abandoned U.S. Naval base.

The base had been established during World War II by agreement between the United States and the British. Macquerupa's location in the southeastern part of the Caribbean had been strategically important for the protection of the Panama Canal, and for the protection of British oil refineries and pitch on the nearby island of Trinidad. At that time, Macquerupa and Trinidad had still been British Crown Colonies.

By the time Macquerupa became self-governing some twenty five years later, relations between the Macquerupian leader and the United States were not very good. There was pressure on the States to leave the island. From the American point of view, the base was no longer needed anyway, and the Navy pulled out when its lease on the land expired.

Renny's uncle, Eddie Brown, tended the snack bar on the beach during the old days when the Yankees were around. He was fond of telling stories about how the Navy kids would be left to run amuck on the beach or in the jungle while their mothers spent their days playing cards and tennis up at the clubhouse. With parents oblivious to the mischief-making of their children, Eddie was always having to bail kids out of one kind of trouble or another.

John David "J.D." Patrick, the donor of Renny's fins, had been one of those Navy kids thirty years ago. He had recently returned to Macquerupa upon hearing that the Navy property was for sale. The island government, now eager to promote tourism and stimulate the island economy, was selling the property for development. J.D. had just bought it. He had long dreamed of building a resort for scuba divers in an exotic place with pristine diving. As far as J.D. was concerned, being able to buy the old Navy clubhouse property was pure luck.

"It'll be the finest dive resort in the entire Caribbean," J.D. bragged. "This island has some of the best reefs around, and the one right here in Coconut Cove is the absolute finest!"

Renny already knew that. Even though he had never been off the island, it was hard for him to imagine how any reef could get any better. In fact, the boy's love for this reef had become so well known among the locals that it had been dubbed as "Renny's Reef."

Renny adjusted his mask and snorkel and put on his fins. Combined with the socks, they were a perfect fit. He attached the catch bag to his waist with a strap and grabbed his speargun. Wading backwards into the surf, he turned the side of his body against each breaking wave. When almost chest deep, he turned and leaned forward in the water, and started kicking.

Diving through swells, Renny became one with the water as he picked up speed. He had never before felt such power from a pair of fins! Skimming over the turtle grass beds toward the patch reefs, he passed over a convoy of conch. Bending at the waist and with quick flicks of his torso, he piked into dive after dive. Gliding like a porpoise, he laughed through his snorkel when an enormous stingray bolted from the sand at his approach. A bar jack scurried after the stingray, looking for scraps of food.

Renny loved the reef and knew it well. He had been skin diving ever since he was a small boy, and lived to be in the water. He was a skilled diver who preferred diving alone. Not that he didn't have friends—they just didn't appreciate the reef the way Renny did.

"Hurry up, fish lover!" they would tease. They were more interested in catching lobsters and spearfishing, and thought Renny was far too obsessed with sea life. They were probably right, Renny thought.

Renny liked to poke around the reef. He would hover in one place for awhile just to see how many fishes would appear after they got used to him being there. Renny found he could see much more life by being patient. The fishes didn't seem to mind Renny's presence, and would just go about their affairs. He felt honored to be accepted by their community.

He did not enjoy spearfishing, and tried to get out of it whenever he could. Not that he was a bad shot—in fact, he was an excellent shot. But after spending so much time on the reef, Renny felt the fishes knew and trusted him. He considered them to be his friends, and felt guilty when he had to show up with a speargun. He was sure to aim carefully so the fish he speared would die instantly, without suffering.

Occasionally his mom would send him out for a special kind of fish—like today, when he was supposed to come back home with a Nassau grouper because it was J.D.'s favorite. He felt especially obligated this time, since it was part of his father's deal for his new fins. Renny tried to remember the last time he saw a Nassau grouper. It had been a long time.

Much of Renny's success with spearfishing had to do with the fact that he could hold his breath for a long time—in fact, he was the breath holding champion among his friends. Not only did they accuse him of loving fish, but they often accused him of actually being half fish. Good-naturedly they would rib him, calling him "Renny the Mer*man*." Renny actually *did* wish he had gills and could stay under water forever. But he didn't have gills—so instead, Renny dreamed about scuba diving.

"Scuba diving is getting to be one of the most popular sports in the States—even the whole world," J.D. had said. "Divers are always looking for unspoiled places to dive. Reefs in other areas are getting too crowded and all dived out. But Macquerupa's reefs—they are totally pristine. Divers will just love it here!"

Macquerupa had been written about in travel and scuba diving magazines recently. Bookings were already coming in, and J.D. expected that business would be picking up steadily. He operated a small dive shop across the road from Cocoa Bay, but planned to move it to Coconut Cove after his resort was built.

Coconut Cove was actually part of Cocoa Bay. On a map it looked as if a bite had been taken out of the far end of the bay. The cove was more protected, and free of the riptides and undertows that often made Cocoa Bay dangerous for swimming.

Renny's Reef was reputed to be the best reef on the island. But as much as Renny wanted to learn to scuba dive, he was not happy about the prospect of having to share his reef with strangers from other countries.

As Renny thought about J.D.'s plans, he kicked harder. Will my reef get all dived out, too? he worried. And what will happen when Macquerupa's reefs get wrecked? Will divers just go somewhere else, just as they are now starting to come to Macquerupa?

Abruptly, Renny stopped kicking as he suddenly realized there was no reef below him anymore.

"What th—!" he blurted through his snorkel. Fighting a rising sense of panic, he almost dropped his speargun. His mind had drifted and he hadn't been paying attention to where he was going.

"Okay, now calm down and breathe normally," he commanded himself. His body obeyed. He looked down again. There was no reef at all below him—

just a bottomless expanse of deep, dark blue. Lifting his head, he whirled his body around to get his bearings.

"Oh, *man*," groaned Renny, spotting a familiar clump of three coconut trees. They marked the point that separated Cocoa Bay from Coconut Cove. He wasn't just beyond the drop-off, he was *way* beyond the drop-off! He would surely be in for trouble at home, and prayed his parents weren't looking. He thought about sharks and currents and being swept off, never to be seen again.

"Okay, okay. Relax. Just be very calm. Kick very smoothly. Think very good thoughts," he instructed himself. "Be calm. Don't act nervous. Don't attract sharks by being nervous. Just be very calm," he repeated over and over to himself.

In a few minutes Renny heaved a sigh of relief as he neared the clump of coconut trees. He was glad to be a strong swimmer, and even happier that he had such powerful fins. Quickly, his confidence returned.

That was way too close, he thought. Maybe these fins make me *too* fast.

As Renny approached the cove, the outline of the reef became visible ahead through the crystal clear water. He had never been out this far before. Slowing down, he hovered above the drop-off.

So this is the drop-off. What's all the fuss and bother about? It looks harmless enough to me... I wonder what it's like down there. Should I check it out—nah, I'd better not.

But Renny continued to hover above the drop-off to look. He guessed the depth to the top of the reef to be around forty or fifty feet.

I'll bet these fins could take me down there in three seconds, he thought to himself. Sighting a reference point on the reef, he drifted for a moment to check the current. It was slight at the surface, but could be different down deeper. Taking a deep breath, Renny piked into a dive, and with a few swift, strong kicks, glided down to the drop-off. Pinching his nose, he blew gently against it to equalize the pressure behind his ears, which squeaked in response as he went deeper. When Renny reached the reef, his eyes popped.

Mama *Yo!* he thought, as he circled slowly to take in the scenery around him.

It's a fairyland out here!

CHAPTER III

The Fairyland

A FOREST of giant feathery, white sea plumes wafted back and forth with the gentle motion of the water. Looking like trees of fringe, the sea plumes clenched massive coral heads with their claw-like roots. In their shade, grunts and snappers drifted back and forth, looking bored.

They're limin', thought Renny, giggling to himself. That is what "hangin' out" was called in Macquerupa.

Everywhere were giant heads of star, flower, and brain corals. They were tinted various shades of yellow-green and tan by algae living within their tissues. These were hard, reef-building corals. Renny had learned about them in school just before Christmas vacation.

Each coral head had been started by one tiny coral animal that had settled from the water and changed into a coral polyp. A special kind of algae moved in, and together the polyp and algae worked to make a skeleton of limestone (chalk) to support the polyp. Otherwise it would just be a mass of jelly.

The polyp would then bud off to form more polyps to start a coral *colony*. Then the other polyps in the colony would bud off, and then *they* would bud off, and the colony would spread outward. As all the polyps in the colony deposited limestone, a coral *clump* was formed and continued to expand. As coral clumps got larger, they became coral *heads*.

An Expanding Coral Colony   *A Coral Clump (Small Coral Head)*

Great Star Coral *(Montastrea cavernosa)*

"But how are *more* coral heads started?" the class had wanted to know. The teacher had replied:

"Oh, that is even *more* fantastic! Not only do coral polyps reproduce by budding off to make colonies, but they also make eggs and spawn! Around or after the full moon at certain times of the year, all the coral colonies of the same specie on a reef all spawn together. The spawn is released into the water by moonlight, floats to the surface, and is carried away by currents under cover of darkness.

"When the spawn are in the open water, they develop into larvae. If the larvae survive and settle in suitable places, they will change into polyps and start new colonies. Then over many thousands of years, coral heads grow and join with other coral heads. And the coral heads are cemented together by *another* type of algae that produces limestone. That is how the massive framework of the coral reef is built."

Renny was amazed at how an entire reef could actually be built by tiny, individual animals.

"It is the most supreme example of teamwork that ever existed," the teacher had said. "Just think of what has been accomplished by individuals working together, with a bit of time and patience."

"Yeah, right! A 'bit' of time? It took for*ever!*" her students had answered.

"But of course it didn't happen overnight," his teacher had said. "Nothing grand ever does."

The reef was an oasis in an otherwise barren environment, providing a food base, as well as homes, for hundreds of other life forms. In the structure of the reef and individual coral heads were nooks and crannies and other hideouts. Creatures took advantage and moved in. The coral heads were like apartment buildings, housing all kinds of fishes and other life.

Some of the more curious of these occupants watched Renny from their hideouts, peering out from behind curtains of algae and soft corals.

It looks like a Dr. Seuss village down here, thought Renny with delight, as he looked all around. He had loved Dr. Seuss books when he was younger—and secretly still did. He started to imagine being in one.

Sand channels shaded by sea plumes separated the coral head apartment houses, looking like winding streets through the fanciful village. Fish flitted from one coral head to another, picking at the soft corals and sponges landscaping them. The fish traffic reminded Renny of the drivers in town. An enormous stoplight parrotfish careened past, trying to shake off a remora.

"Get off my tail!" the fish seemed to snarl. Renny giggled again. He was beginning to feel like part of a Dr. Seuss world.

Renny surfaced for another breath, returning this time to a sand channel as it became a canyon-like sand *chute*. He followed the sand chute until it spilled over the drop-off onto the reef wall.

At the drop-off, corals thrived as the current swept in abundant amounts of plankton from the open ocean. Here was the reef crest, where the towering coral heads got so massive they fused with neighboring coral heads to form umbrellas, tunnels and grottos. Some of the sand chutes disappeared into these grottos and emerged farther down on the reef wall.

Hundreds of dark blue and gold iridescent creole wrasse parted around Renny in an unending stream as they looped over the reef crest, back down along the wall, and then back up again. Great masses of lacy gorgonian soft corals hung from the reef wall as it cascaded into the depths. Renny looked up to catch a huge manta ray gliding overhead, its wings smoothly flapping against the gentle current.

Annoyed again by his need to breathe, Renny surfaced for a breath, and hurried back down again—this time to the reef wall itself. Soon his sharp eyes spotted two long antennae sticking out from a crevice, and Renny remembered that he was supposed to be catching dinner. Sneaking up on the lobster, he swiftly reached in to grab it before it could snap back into its hole.

"Gotcha!" said Renny through his snorkel. He took

Creole Wrasse on the Wall

pride in not needing a tickle stick to catch lobsters. The lobster was huge, and would easily be enough for two people. Renny carefully stuffed the protesting crustacean into his catch bag as he spiraled up for another breath, surveying the area for shark and barracuda on his way to the surface.

Renny glided back down again and found a sand channel at the top of the reef, landward of the reef crest. He set down his catch bag and speargun in the sand while he continued to look for more lobster.

Returning to his catch bag with his third lobster, Renny's eye caught a slight movement to the side. Turning his head, Renny found himself looking into the bright, clear eyes of a large fish with brown and white stripes. It had fat lips and a characteristic tuning fork pattern on its forehead. Under its eyes were · little black spots, and near the tail was a large black spot. It paled slightly but otherwise showed no fear of the boy. It just looked intently at Renny, as if curious to see who was responsible for catching the lobsters. It was the most beautiful Nassau grouper Renny had ever seen.

Wow, thought Renny.

Whoa, thought the grouper.

With the lobster still squirming in his hand, Renny remained motionless until his lungs called for air again. Cursing them, Renny surfaced for a breath. He started to head back down again, when suddenly, his lobster was ripped from his hand.

"What th—!" Caught completely off guard, Renny almost inhaled sea water as he shot up for the surface, swinging around just in time to glimpse a huge, silver barracuda making off with his catch. Renny sputtered and gasped for air as he broke the surface. It took several breaths before he could settle down enough to inspect his hand. It smarted, but it wasn't bleeding. He could put up with the pain as long as it wasn't bleeding. He was thankful it hadn't been a shark.

Renny was more surprised than frightened. Normally barracudas would just hang back and observe people, and were were not aggressive. He must've thought I was feedin' him, thought Renny. But who would be feedin' the barries out here, he wondered as he kicked back down again.

The grouper was still there as Renny returned to the bottom. The boy gently settled back down on his belly next to his speargun and catch bag, where his first two lobsters quarreled in their new, very close quarters. Renny ignored them. His eyes focused on the grouper.

Hey there, big fella, thought the boy, creeping closer to the grouper.

Hey, Buck, thought the grouper, watching Renny.

Renny's hand inched toward his speargun. His fingers wrapped around the shaft, and slowly his hand drew the weapon toward him. He pulled back on the rubber sling, taking aim on the big fish.

Hey! thought the grouper, cocking his body to the side. His stripes disappeared as he paled to match the color of the sand bottom.

Renny froze. Then he blinked hard. Now where did that grouper go? Renny blinked again. The fish was gone. Slowly, Renny reversed his draw on the sling. He lazily spiraled up to the surface, keeping his eyes peeled for the grouper.

Where did he go? thought Renny again, as he circled back down toward the sand channel. Stopping to hover above the reef, he slowly rotated to survey the area around him. He kept his eyes unfocused to better detect movement.

Suddenly, there was the grouper again, sitting quietly on his tail. He had been watching every move

the boy had made. Renny's focus quickly sharpened on the fish.

The grouper started to swim away. He turned back to look at Renny and then started following a sand chute. The grouper again stopped, turned back, and waited for Renny.

Renny followed the grouper. Staying calm, he maintained a safe distance so he wouldn't alarm the fish. The grouper moved slowly, swinging his tail gently from side to side. Then he turned back again to look at Renny. But the boy needed another breath. The grouper waited for Renny, and then continued down the sand chute, until abruptly, it came to an end. With one last look back at Renny, the grouper vanished behind a massive clump of brown tube sponges.

Curious, Renny drifted toward the sponges. In response, tiny fish fry retreated into them. Behind the clump of sponges a thicket of sea plumes clenching the sides of the chute canopied the sand bottom. Through the branches, Renny could see a long, dark crevice. The coral heads on each side of the chute had branched out so much that they had fused together to form a grotto with a narrow opening.

Renny hesitated. Then he glided under the sea plumes and peered inside the darkened grotto. His eye caught the glint of hundreds of tiny silversides, shimmering in shafts of sunlight that dappled the cavern's interior. Suddenly, Renny felt pulled into the grotto by an unknown force. Cautiously, he slid through the opening.

CHAPTER IV

The Grotto

A SENSE of magic and calm infused Renny. Looking up, he could see where light entered the grotto ceiling through small scattered openings, softened by the lacy silhouettes of soft corals. Renny could catch glimpses of fishes as they darted in and out of the portals.

On the bottom of the grotto were shells and pieces of coral rubble that had accumulated in low spots of the sand. In contrast to the reef outside, very little of anything grew inside, except for little patches of green algae that were able to catch what little light was allowed into the cavern.

A fat green moray as long as Renny slithered out of a dark crevice, startling Renny as it brushed up against his arm. The eel's supple, slippery body felt smooth and silky.

It's so soft! Renny thought, surprised.

The eel then disappeared through the school of silversides. They parted in unison to let the eel pass, then came back together again. As Renny followed the eel, the swarm of silversides parted around him, too. They were as tiny as goldfish. Renny could hear them crackle, sounding like a wad of cellophane as

they moved in complete unison, back and forth—
always turning at once as if they were being open
and shut like a set of Venetian blinds.

This is fantastic! thought Renny.

He turned back through the school again and hovered in its midst. Holding out his arm, he slowly
waved it back and forth through the water. The tiny
fish parted around his arm each time he waved it
through the mass.

Catching the light of another opening, Renny
turned and glided toward it. This one was larger
than the entrance. Surrounded by a lush growth of
black gorgonians, this was where the sand chute
exited the grotto on the reef wall. There sat the grouper, just inside the opening, perched on top of an
old wooden barrel sticking out of the sand.

Renny's eyebrows shot up. What a strange place for a barrel! But he forgot the barrel, and focused on the grouper. What a fish. So relaxed, and obviously content with his life.

From his perch on the barrel, the grouper had the most sensational view of the reef wall and all life on it. Renny dropped down on his belly in the sand next to the barrel, and gazed along with the grouper at one of the most beautiful sights he'd ever seen in his life. It took away Renny's breath.

The endless parade of creole wrasse streamed past in front of them. A pair of enormous black and gold French angelfish picked their way across purple sea fans as big as tables. Incredible stands of black gorgonians forested the wall, punctuated here and there by barrel sponges big enough to hold people. A giant hawksbill turtle appeared out of nowhere and waved before it disappeared again.

Nice view, hey? thought the grouper.

Sure is, thought Renny, taking in the view. This has to be the prettiest place on Earth.

You bet your fins, it's a good place to be. Even better than Earth—it is heaven to me! thought the grouper as he gazed at his territory on the wall.

It sure is, thought Renny, wistfully.

Sure is, thought the grouper.

Mesmerized by the activity on the wall, Renny thought, I could stay here forever.

Yeah, thought the fish.

Sitting together in silence, they watched and thought.

Suddenly, Renny twitched.

"Hey, *wait* a minute!" he blurted, bubbles pouring from his mouth. He sprang from his belly to his knees. If his hair hadn't already been standing on end from being under water, it would surely have done so now. He looked down and patted his chest. Then he grabbed his right arm. He grabbed his left leg. Then he waved his hands in front of his mask. Yes, he was really there, all right. *But what was happening?*

Was he chatting with a fish? Nah! This conversation couldn't be happening. It had to be his imagination. He had never doubted that fish communicate with each other, but was this fish really conversing with him? Can fish really do that?

Sure we can, thought the grouper. He looked at Renny with his right eye.

Aw, come on, thought Renny, this can't be real.

Just then, Renny realized he hadn't taken a breath for what had seemed like a very long time. Alarmed, he pinched himself again.

Did I drown? Am I dead?

"Whoa." The grouper turned toward Renny. "Now why would you think a thing like that?"

"This is too weird. I don't have to breathe. I feel fine. In fact, I feel great. I feel better than I have in my whole entire life! And here I am, yakking with a fish. What is this? Reef magic? There is no reef magic. This is too weird. I am *out* of here!" Renny turned around.

"There's nothing to fear, when you're in my den. But you can go out the way you came in." The grouper motioned to Renny with a pectoral fin.

"Oh yeah, and fish-poet, too," muttered Renny through his teeth, as he hurried back through the grotto.

"Fish *like* to rhyme from time to time. So what? Enjoy it. And don't slam the sea plumes on your way out," Renny heard.

Renny paused and glared back.

"What?"

The green moray disappeared into a hole in the grotto wall.

Finding the opening through which he'd entered the grotto, Renny glided back through the sea plumes, past the yellow sponges, and into the open sand chute. He was relieved when he felt the urge to breathe again.

The grouper followed Renny to make sure the boy could find his way back to the door—then rushed to a window to watch Renny as he surfaced.

What an odd one, thought the grouper.

"Yo! I *am* still alive!" Renny yelled out to the sky upon surfacing. He turned back and started toward the beach. But I guess there'll be no grouper for dinner tonight, he thought. He felt a twinge of guilt for not coming back with J.D.'s favorite meal.

But you've got lobsters. What more could you want? thought the grouper, watching from his window as the boy sped away.

The lobsters! Renny suddenly remembered. He had almost forgotten them. The sand chute was still below him. He followed it back to the sand channel, where he spotted the wiggling catch bag. His speargun still lay in the sand near it. Renny grabbed it, along with his catch, and quickly surfaced again.

Keeping the sand channel in sight from the surface, Renny snorkeled back toward shore. When he got to the patch reefs, the sand channel merged with other channels, becoming the sand flats more familiar to Renny.

Hey, wait a minute, he thought. Something made him stop and look around. Then he recognized a giant head of brain coral nearby, and knew he could find this spot again. Diving back down, he gathered pieces of coral rubble, arranged them in the shape of a big "G", and resurfaced.

Renny poked his head out of the water to find that he still was not far from the point that separated Coconut Cove from Cocoa Bay. If he went through the bay, he could get home faster. Normally he avoided the bay, as there were often dangerous rip tides and undertows. But with his new fins, he was sure he could get through anything at all.

Renny turned into the bay and sped toward the beach, kicking hard. He felt as if he had been away for an eternity and was afraid his parents would be worried. Back in shallow water, he pulled down his face mask, doffed his fins, and waded to shore.

Several fishermen working on fish traps nodded as he hurried past them with his spear gun and bag of lobsters.

"Hey, man," they said.

"Yeah, man," he mumbled, not looking up.

CHAPTER V

Christmas Dinner

RENNY, his parents and J.D. ate on the Thomases'
front porch overlooking Cocoa Bay. It was just
after sunset. The lights of a cruise ship came
into view, soon followed by the faint rhythm of
calypso music floating to shore on the breeze.

"Wonder which boat it is," said J.D..

A pleasant evening sea breeze had picked up. The
diners were full. Mrs. Thomas had made a lime-butter sauce for the lobster, roasted the pork, prepared
stuffed eggplant, and made hops—yeast rolls. Everything was delicious. They all agreed as they licked
and wiped their fingers that there was hardly anything that tasted better than fresh lobster dipped in
lime-butter sauce.

"Except for maybe a nice big, fat, juicy Nassau
grouper dipped in lime-butter sauce," J.D. added.

Renny stiffened and looked down at his plate.

"Oh, we were hopin' Renny could find one for you this afternoon. But I guess you didn't see one, did you, dear?" said Mrs. Thomas, patting Renny's hand.

Renny opened his mouth to speak.

"They *are* gettin' harder to find," his mother continued. "But not to worry, we should have some soon enough. My grouper is the best on the island." Mrs. Thomas was looking forward to being able to offer fresh grouper in her cafe again.

"Grouper Moon," said Mr. Thomas, looking at the waxing moon. It hung low over the horizon.

"What's Grouper Moon?" asked J.D..

"That's when all the Nassaus 're roein'. They're easy to catch then 'cause they're all grouped together and have other things on their minds. The rest of the year they're hard to nab 'cause they're loners. Every now and then someone'll bring one in on a spear. But they're gettin' awful hard to find anymore. They're gettin' real hard to find."

"They're not as big as they used to be, either," added Mrs. Thomas. She was thinking about how many servings she could get out of one fish.

"I don't remember anything about Grouper Moon when we lived here. But then I probably wouldn't, being a Yankee," J.D. said. Then he added, "Grouper sure was gettin' expensive back home in Florida. But people still couldn't get enough of it."

"That's because it tastes so good," Mrs. Thomas said. "Irresistible!" She was thinking about new grouper recipes to try. Lime-butter sauce was always a real hit with the diners, but she was starting to get bored with it.

Mr. Thomas said, "They say the fish packing companies are paying top dollar for Nassaus now. Around here that means every fisherman and his brother'll be out there off Rocky Point trying to cash in. That's where all the groupers gather. Every fisherman from the island'll be there. The catch was down last year, and there's talk of doubling efforts this year to make up for it."

"What are they gonna do?" J.D. asked.

"Well, for one thing, they're gonna use a lot of traps. They're not supposed to set traps inside the spawnin' grounds, so they'll just put 'em right outside the grounds. Try to catch the fish comin' and goin'. And they'll bait their lines with live sardines. Groupers just looove sardines. And some're even gonna go down on scuba and spear."

"Are they trained on scuba?" John asked, concerned.

"Nah. There's usually a few accidents because they stay down too long and get the bends. That's what happened to the Henry boy a coupla years ago. But it doesn't seem to make any difference. Especially to the young men. They just think they are invincible."

"I used to like to spearfish out in the cove when I was a kid," said J.D.. "We saw Nassaus all the time. But they were pretty smart fish and could give you a real challenge. Seems like you'd take aim on one and then he'd just dissolve right before your eyes. Then you'd turn around and find him laughing at you from a hole in the coral behind you. But they could be pretty friendly too. If you didn't have a spear they might even follow you around like a puppy dog. You could even pet 'em. They sure are ugly buggers, though."

"They're *not* ugly," Renny absently mumbled. Everyone looked at him.

"What'd you say?" his dad said.

"Huh?" Renny said, startled.

"Seems like you weren't with us there. Where were your thoughts?" Mr. Thomas said, kindly.

"Oh, I doh know."

"Say Renny, do you ever see any Nassaus out there on the reef?" J.D. asked, stretching back in his chair. He clasped his hands behind his head.

Renny hesitated.

"Nah," he said, getting up from the table. "Hey, I'm not feelin' so good. Maybe I should go lay down or somethin'."

"It wasn't the eggplant, was it, honey?" Mrs. Thomas said, looking at Renny with concern.

"Nah. I doh know. Maybe I'm jus' really tired," said the boy. He couldn't stop thinking about the grotto and the grouper, and just wanted to be alone.

"Say, Renny, have you had a chance to try out those fins yet?" J.D. asked him.

Renny had forgotten to thank J.D.. He slapped the side of his head with the palm of his hand.

"Oh, *yeah*. They're the greatest! Thanks." Renny walked over to shake J.D.'s hand. "Sorry I couldn't get you a Nassau."

"You're welcome! But don't worry about not getting me a Nassau. Sounds like I'll have more than I can eat soon enough," said J.D..

"Yeah, I guess so," said Renny.

"Say, I'm going to need some help down at the dive shop soon when the tourists start coming in. Are you interested?" J.D. said.

"Yeah, sure," said Renny, looking down.

"Well, maybe we can talk about it later if you're not feeling so good now. Why don't you stop by the shop later on this week when you're feeling better and we can talk about it then."

"Cool," said Renny.

Mr. and Mrs. Thomas beamed.

"You'd better go get some rest now, dear," said Mrs. Thomas.

Renny went to his room. He lay down on his bed with his hands clasped behind his head and stared out into nowhere.

CHAPTER VI

The Changeover

EARLY the next morning a red coral crab tee tered lightly on its tiptoes in the sand bottom of the grotto, searching for bits of dung. Absorbed in activity, the scavenger skittered sideways, zigzagging back and forth and side to side in little stops and starts. Unaware of a set of enormous lips nearby, the crab went about its business—back and forth, side to side, start, stop, start, stop.

Above the big lips were two large, sleepy eyes. They took turns, lazily following the movements of the busy crustacean. The left eye watched when the crab was to the left, then the right eye took over and watched when the crab moved to the right. Back and forth. Closer. Side to side. Closer. And closer— until the big lips opened and shot forward with a wide yawn, and the mouth clamped shut. The unlucky decapod was gone.

Gulp!

Suddenly, all fins sprang out at once as the groggy fish was jolted fully awake. He shuddered as the twitching crab passed through his innards.

"Whoa," groaned Cooper the grouper, in a low,

gravelly voice, as he coughed and sputtered, "A big one. Oh! Oh, my belly." He shuddered again.

Even though he had been hungrier than usual lately, this display of gluttony was not normal for Cooper. As a Nassau grouper, he was a gentle-hearted fish with good manners, and preferred to ease into his day with just a quick little bite. He would get more serious about nutrition in good time, but first he preferred to wake up and gather his wits. Then he liked to catch up with all the happenings about his territory on the reef. Having to deal with a belly-ache was not Cooper's idea of a good way to start his day.

The grouper, however, quickly forgot his troubles, as his eye caught a soft gleam of light through an opening to his grotto. His fins shot up.

"The changeover!" he gasped.

With a boom, he bolted for his favorite opening overlooking his territory on the reef drop-off. Watching the morning changeover was a daily ritual for Cooper. He had almost missed it.

This was the time when fish on the night shift would come in from their hunts to settle down for the day. The day shift would then emerge from *their* sleeping spots, and soon the reef would bustle with activity.

Cooper loved watching this process from beginning to end. Being top dog of his territory, Cooper felt somewhat responsible in knowing that all residents were in from the night and accounted for. Some would have to travel to the patch reefs or the turtle grass beds to hunt. Others would go out into open water. Cooper worried about them having to leave his territory. Most returned. Some did not.

Sometimes newcomers would arrive to set up housekeeping. The grouper liked to know when this happened as well. But more than anything else, Cooper simply enjoyed hanging back quietly, taking in the activity around him.

He was thankful to be a grouper who was content to just hang around. He pitied other fish who constantly had to be flitting here and there. They could never relax and just enjoy life on the reef.

Cooper loved his life on the reef. How every creature—big and small, simple and complex, living or dead—contributed to the symphony of life on the coral reef was a constant marvel to him.

His bellyache forgotten, Cooper settled into his favorite spot on top of his barrel. He leaned back on his tail to enjoy the changeover. He was relieved that he hadn't missed much of it.

"Heya, Coop." It was one of the bluestriped grunts passing by, rejoining the groups of grunts already in for the day. They were gathered under their favorite sea plumes.

"Hey, yourself," Cooper called back.

A sea urchin with long, black spines settled into a dark crevice in the coral. Several spindly red brittle stars disappeared into the folds of a giant barrel sponge.

The big eyes and squirrelfish found their usual hangouts under dark ledges in the wall. Cooper always got them mixed up because both species were red and looked so much alike. They ignored Cooper.

They didn't appreciate being confused with each other.

A delicate basket star waved its lacy arms in greeting. It had been straining plankton from the water, and was rolling up its vast network of branching arms into tight little balls. Cooper watched in awe as the tight little balls then hunkered down into an unappetizing wiry wad for the day. It clung to the gorgonian with its roots.

Crabs and lobsters quietly backed into their favorite nooks and crannies to hide. They preferred not to be noticed by the grouper.

Coral colonies that had been blooming during the night began to retract their tentacles into the skeletons of their polyps.

When everyone was in, all the tiny little cardinalfish, who had been hovering above the reef eating plankton, sank down into the reef. This signified the end of the night shift. Now everything would be quiet for a short time.

This was the part Cooper liked best—when the reef was still. As much as he enjoyed watching the reef activity, he was, as a grouper, a loner. This time of peace and quiet was important to Cooper. It was the time he reserved just for himself. Without it, his day didn't seem right. He knew the quiet wouldn't last long, and didn't want to miss a minute of it.

There was an evening changeover, too—a mirror image of the morning process—when the day shift settled down and the night shift took over again. But that was a more active hunting time for Cooper. There was no time for personal reflection then.

"Ahhhhhh..." said Cooper, shifting on his tail. "It fills me inside from my fins to my nose, this feeling of gladness, inside me it grows. How I do love my spot on this reef in the sea. Me oh my, yes—it's a good place to be!" He was soon lost in pleasant thoughts, when—

Crrrunnnch!

—the grouper's fins all sprang out at once.

"Huh?!? My oh me. There it goes—the peace that *did* fill me from fins to my nose. The spell is now broken. Oh my—what commotion breaks forth near my spot on this reef in the ocean?"

Crrrunnnch!

"I should have known," sighed Cooper when he saw Sam, a parrotfish. Sam had just shaken free from his cocoon of mucous and had started in on his own day, chomping on coral. Sam didn't have a territory; he just wandered around, chowing down on everyone else's coral. Then he would just move on without so much as a "How-are-you-ma'am-my-name-is-Sam."

The normally tolerant Nassau grouper watched, growing more annoyed, as the beautiful parrotfish thoughtlessly scraped big chunks out of the coral, leaving ugly, white patches.

What nerve. Just because he's gorgeous, he thinks he can get away with anything, thought Cooper. The grouper became indignant.

"Hey! Cut it out over there! Go on, do your munching in some other place. I'm sick of your crunching! You're wrecking my coral. You're being quite pesty. You're making a mess, and I'm getting quite testy!"

The parrotfish paused and gave the testy fish a blank look. Then he said, "So what's up *your* gullet, my dear esteemed grouper? My, my, you're cranky. That's not like our Cooper. Unruffle your scales! I'm just doing my job. I'm making sand—and don't call me a slob."

The parrotfish quickly forgot Cooper and went back to his munching and crunching.

Cooper's heart sank. The parrotfish had a point. It wasn't like the grouper to be so irritable. The normally gentle-hearted fish started to brood. He didn't feel right about being irritable.

"What's going on here? What causes this blight? Something's not fitting. My bones don't feel right."

His meditation time was spoiled. Ordinarily laid-back, Cooper now felt restless and began to wander. Little fishes, surprised to see a wandering Nassau grouper, quickly scattered.

A small school of banded butterflyfish flitted from one coral head to another, picking at algae with tiny mouths on their pointy little snouts. They ignored the big grouper, who scowled at them.

"Pick pick pick. Do you suppose, just one would pick beyond his nose?"

A nervous sergeant major darted back and forth, guarding its purple mass of eggs. Cooper paid no attention. His eye caught sight of a pair of angelfish, nipping on sponges.

"Yuck," said Cooper in disgust. "I'd rather eat crabs than spicules, any time."

The thought of crabs made Cooper hungry again. A popular feeding spot on the reef was on the side of the bay, around some concrete pilings. It had been a long time since Cooper had wandered so far away from his territory. But he knew there would be plenty of crabs there, and right now he was in a crabby mood.

He loved crab. He ate other things, too, like small fishes and lobsters—but crab was Cooper's personal favorite. Choosing a sandy spot in the shelter of a piling, he lay motionless. It wasn't long before he spotted one.

"Mmmmmm....I have a feeling. Yes, I have a hunch, that my belly wants this little morsel for brunch." He chuckled to himself as he became motionless in anticipation of the ambush.

The little morsel skittered sideways, back and forth, while the hungry grouper waited patiently until it was near his mouth. Then, *whoosh!* Cooper's mouth opened and shot out, sucked in the crab and clamped back shut again—all in an instant. The crab never knew what hit it. Cooper preferred it that way. Gulp!

"Whoa," said the grouper contentedly, as his brunch went down his gullet—this time, more smoothly.

"Wow!" Cooper heard.

"Whoa! What was that?" Cooper's fins all sprang out as he looked around. Then he leaned to his side and looked up. He was being watched from above.

His fins went back down. Not to worry. It was Buck, the odd one who had followed him into his grotto. Cooper had heard other fishes call humans "Buck." Cooper liked the name, and thought it fit this boy quite nicely.

Renny hovered quietly at the surface, watching the grouper. Then he dived down and lay on his belly in the sand, face to face with Cooper.

"So you'd like to see me do that again, hey?" the grouper thought. He had to agree with Buck that his method of catching dinner was pretty slick. Even if he said so himself.

The boy went back up to the surface and hovered, waiting for the grouper to vacuum in another bite. Cooper settled in the sand again and obliged when the next crab came close enough.

"Mmmmm, I do love a good crab." Cooper sank back on his tail to enjoy his treat. He found himself enjoying showing off in front of Buck. But soon he became aware that the boy was no longer there.

Bummer, thought Cooper. He had started to enjoy having him around. He pondered this.

"Whoa! Hold on, here. I'm a *grouper*," he said, suddenly. He was surprised at feeling bothered by the human's departure. Groupers were loners. They weren't supposed to need others around them. And they weren't show-offs, either.

Whoa, thought Cooper. He started to wander again, and lost himself in his brooding.

"It eats at my bone, that something's not right—a feeling has grown. I prefer solace, and like my spot, only. But, this morning I'm restless—I think I feel *lonely*."

The grouper stopped dead in his tracks.

A lonely loner?

"Whoa! Oh, *my!*" Cooper the grouper gasped.

CHAPTER VII

Getting Ready

RENNY faintly heard his name over the lapping of sea water against the nearby rocks. He was snorkeling around the old pilings on the side of Cocoa Bay, engrossed by a Nassau grouper's feeding technique. Certain it was the same grouper he had met at the drop-off, Renny thought it strange that the grouper would be this far away from his grotto.

"*Ren*ton, come quickly!" Renny heard again, more clearly this time. It was his father was calling from the beach. Renny reluctantly turned away from the pilings and headed for shore. When it was too shallow to swim, he removed his fins and walked out of the water.

Renny's dad was on the beach with Uncle Eddie and several other fishermen working on fish traps. They were deep in conversation, casting worried glances toward the northeast sky.

"Come, len' hand wi' dese!" Mr. Thomas said to his son as Renny approached the group. They were hauling traps to the boats.

"Whatcha gonna do wit alla dese?" Renny asked, as his dad motioned for him to take one end of a trap to carry. Renny already knew, of course. Mr. Thomas gave his son a funny look.

"Wadda yuh mean, man? Is Grouper Moon!" answered one of the fishermen. It was Buster Henry.

"Yeah?" said Renny.

"In jus' a couple a days, alla dem ugly, yummy Nassaus alla gonna be right where dey is easy to catch! Alla we do is put out de traps an' so, an' bait de lines, an' haul dem in. Haul, an' haul, an' haul!" said Buster.

"Dey *not* ugly," said Renny.

"Oh no, Nassaus big, an' dey fat. An' dey ugly. But dey *sweet!*" replied Buster.

Renny said nothing. He looked at all the traps and thought about his grouper. His shoulders sagged.

Buster and his brother, Andrew, had moved to

Macquerupa a few years ago from a neighboring island, where the fishing had gone bad. Andrew had gotten the bends two years before while spearfishing the Nassau grouper aggregation. He had survived that incident. But the next month when he was spearfishing a different grouper aggregation, he never returned to his boat. Andrew had not been trained on scuba, and had used no gauges. He had ignored advice about safety from more experienced divers, even after his first accident.

The islanders speculated for weeks about his disappearance. "He get de pressure sickness again... mebbe he shark meat... de current probally carry he off..."

In spite of what had happened to his brother, Buster was still more concerned about catching and selling all the fish he could. It didn't seem to matter to him how he did it. Many of the other fishermen thought Buster was too greedy, but put up with him, anyway.

A long length of wire mesh lay on the beach. Several men were repairing holes in it. Renny walked over to them.

"What's dis?" Renny said as they passed by them.

"Dissis gonna be de holdin' pen! When de traps and de lines get full, we does empty de fish into de pen, to keep dem live and fresh till we bring dem all in," replied one of the men.

Renny had just watched a Nassau ambush his meal by stealth and a fast jaw. The grouper took just what he needed, instantly, before its prey could even know what had hit it. Renny wondered what the groupers must think when they get lured into traps. Or when they struggle bleeding on a spear.

"Renny, doh drop de trap so!" warned Mr. Thomas.

"Sorry," said Renny, absently.

"Easy now," said his dad, as they lowered the trap into his boat. It was one of many long open wooden skiffs with peeling paint, called pirogues, that lined the beach under coconut trees. Renny wondered if the Nassaus had any clue at all about the armada that would soon greet them at their annual spawning reunion.

"Hey, y'all!" they heard from behind and turned around. It was J.D. emerging from the surf, fully clad in scuba gear. He waved in greeting as he trudged toward the group, carrying his fins.

"Hey," said Renny.

"How was your dive?" said Mr. Thomas.

"In-ca-*red*-ible! You do have to be careful getting out, though and not go in front of the red flags marking the bad currents. But this has got to be the best diving in the entire Caribbean. I don't know how this island has escaped the diving world for so long. It is absolutely breathtaking out there," said J.D.. He turned toward the water and studied the bay.

"J.D., have you met my uncle?" Mr. Thomas said.

"I don't believe I have yet had the pleasure," said J.D., sticking out his right hand to shake Uncle Eddie's.

"J.D. is the one who bought the old Navy property at the cove. He wants to build a scuba diving resort," said Mr. Thomas.

"Yuh doh say!" said Uncle Eddie. "Well, it's about time somebody did something with that 'ole heap of rubble up there."

"Yeah, when I was a kid that old heap of rubble was a pretty cool place," said J.D.. "I'd like to rebuild it the way it was thirty years ago."

"Mama *Yo!*" exclaimed Eddie, slapping his leg. "Yuh mean you were one of those Yankees runnin' wild while your mama played cards up at the clubhouse?"

J.D. squinted his eyes and looked at the old man more closely. "Eddie?"

"A-a! Yeah, man, I'm old Eddie. Except now I'm real old," he chuckled. "And which one of those crazy kids were you?"

"John Patrick."

"John Patrick," repeated Eddie. "John Patrick. John David Patrick. Oh, my. I remember your mama flyin' down those steps yellin', 'John David *Patrick!*' You were so full of beans that you were jet propelled. No one could ever keep up wit yuh! Always off somewhere in the jungle, or way out there on the reef, always a worryin' everybody. One time they thought you were swept off to Mexico. Oh, that was a scare, all right. We had every boat we could find out there looking for yuh. Then it turns out you're hidin' out there on the point," said Eddie, pointing to the point where the clump of three coconut trees stood in the distance. "Yuh said you were waitin' for pirates to come back for treasure they'd left behind."

J.D. grinned. "Yeah, that was me all right. I'm afraid I gave my poor mother more gray hairs than she deserved, God rest her soul."

"Oh?" asked Eddie.

"I'm afraid she and Dad both passed away last year," said J.D..

"Oh, I'm real sorry," said Eddie.

"Yeah, it was a shame. They were in a car accident. But in their wills they said I should take whatever there was and use it to follow my heart. Funny how out of a real tragedy can come the most unexpected diamonds. So here I am, back where my heart has always been. I must be the luckiest man alive," said J.D..

"A-a," said Uncle Eddie. "So what'll be your plans, then?"

"Well, first I want to build a little hotel just like the old officers club. Complete with the veranda so people can sit out with the parrots and enjoy that magnificent view out over the cove. I want to redo the grounds going down the hill to the beach. The retaining walls should still be intact, the way all the rest of the old concrete stuff has survived. And have a tree house in the old mango tree for the kids, and the grandest of Easter egg hunts—the way we used to have," said J.D..

"Yeah, and you'll have smashed eggs smothered with ants all over the place the way yuh used to have. Yuh wouldn't believe the messes you kids used to leave behind from those egg hunts."

J.D. laughed. "And I want to rebuild the changing rooms on the beach," he said, with an elbow-nudge to Eddie's arm.

"A-a, you youngsters always had a good time in those changin' rooms," grinned Eddie, slapping his leg again. "Always spyin' on the teenagers and scar-in' 'em out! That always kept 'em in line," he said with a wink to J.D..

Mr. Thomas said, "How're yuh gonna do the dive shop part, J.D.? That's gonna be an awful long flight of stairs to be carryin' heavy tanks up and down."

"Oh, I'm gonna hire Renny here to do that," J.D. said, with a straight face.

"A-a, man!" laughed Uncle Eddie, slapping Renny on the back.

J.D. continued, "Actually, I want to do something with the old pilings. There's enough of a platform left and if it checks out okay for soundness, I'd like to put a dive platform on it—with an air station, and a place to store tanks and gear. And a place to park a few dive boats."

Renny's eyes opened wide. "A *few* dive boats?"

"Yes sir, I want Renny's Reef to be the best-equipped dive resort in the Caribbean!" J.D. answered.

Renny's face fell. He thought about his reef. He thought about strangers invading what he had always regarded as his own. And he was sorely reminded of that fact that even though it had his name on it, it indeed was not his own reef.

"What do you think, Renny? I could teach you to scuba dive, and you could be my number one dive guide!" said J.D., with a gentle punch to Renny's arm.

J.D. stopped smiling when he saw Renny's face.

"Hey, did I say something wrong?" he asked.

Renny hesitated before answering, "Nah."

But Renny was thinking, Yeah, that's pretty cool,

you getting to do what you always wanted to do. But your mom and dad had to die first. I always wanted to scuba dive, and never thought I'd ever get to. Now all-of-a-sudden I have the chance. But I don't want my reef getting wrecked.

J.D. studied Renny intently. Mr. Thomas looked at his son with love, and Uncle Eddie patted Renny's shoulder.

CHAPTER VIII

Dem Bones

I T was another morning. Cooper sat perched on his barrel, as usual, watching the changeover at daybreak. But this time, he wasn't daydreaming pleasant thoughts about his life on the reef. Now his thoughts were of Sadie, another Nassau grouper, whose territory was next to his.

He and Sadie didn't hang out together, being solitary sorts of fish—as groupers are supposed to be. They were content to stay in their own territories, but every now and then they would encounter each other. When that happened, Sadie's color pattern would change, getting dark on the top and white on her belly, and Cooper's pattern would intensify. They might show each other their teeth. Then that would be the end of it before Sadie turned aside and swam back to her business.

That Cooper was now thinking of Sadie was a new experience for the grouper. His innards twisted and turned. He was all mixed up. He didn't know what to do with these new emotions. One minute he'd be light-headed, and the next he'd be glum. Then he'd be confused. Things made no sense.

Now he was restless. He went back into his grotto and began darting back and forth through the darkened cavern. His tail swished side to side behind him with ever-increasing speed.

The green moray poked his head out of a crevice and studied the nervous grouper.

That fish is getting stranger by the minute, he thought. Then he said aloud, "Hey Coop, you're gonna wilt your gills if you keep that up!"

"Huh?" Cooper stopped, but his gills continued to heave rapidly.

"You are driving me nuts!" snapped the moray. Then he said, nicely this time, "Why don't you go out and get all cleaned up? It'll make you feel better." He was hoping to get rid of the fidgety fish.

And without knowing why, that suddenly seemed like a good idea to Cooper, and he found himself being taken to the cleaners. As he arrived, there were already a few other fish ahead of him waiting to be cleaned. He got in line. They all turned to look in surprise at the Nassau grouper. He was humming.

Before Cooper knew it, it was his turn. When the fairy basslets and juvenile hogfish saw Cooper, they yelled to the gobies. The gobies then yelled to the Pederson shrimps, who were taking a break. Blennies popped their heads out of old worm holes in the coral to see what the commotion was all about.

"Hey everybody, Coop's here!"

The cleaners all liked Cooper. They felt his gentleness and good will, and always took pride in making the grouper look and smell good. But this time, there was something different about Cooper—something new. What could it be?

He was...well, now he was giddy.

"Ooooooh, maybe he's finally got a gal!" giggled one of the gobies.

The Nassau grouper moved into position. He flared his gill covers and opened his mouth as wide as he could, being careful not to suck in the tiny cleaners. Rolling back his eyes, he relaxed, keeping his mouth wide open. More than a dozen cleaners appeared and hopped aboard the grouper.

The cleaners worked extra hard this time, taking great care with their favorite customer. Two cleaner gobies, bright with black and yellow stripes, darted inside Cooper's mouth and gently picked away, working their way from his teeth, through the mouth, and out through the gills. Several nimble shrimp worked on the grouper's eyes and snout, while the tiny hogfish nibbled at scales toward the rear of the big fish.

Tiny purple and gold fairy basslets darted back and forth, to and from the grouper. They weren't really cleaners, but they looked so much like the purple and gold hogfish, they had decided they were hogfish, too. They did whatever the hogfish did.

Cooper was in a trance. The cleaners didn't have to worry about getting eaten by him, or any other fishes they cleaned. They provided a valuable service, and they knew it. The cleaners fed on dead skin, parasites, and any other scummy things that could cause disease. But it also felt very good, too— almost like getting a massage.

When the cleaners were finished with Cooper, they swam back to admire their work. The Pederson shrimp scratched their heads with their pinchers. The gobies tipped back on their tails. The fairy basslets and hogfish darted back and forth, looking at Cooper from different angles. Something was missing.

Then the hogfish swam over to a nearby sea fan and whispered to Henry, a neck crab, who had been watching the whole process. The crab had a little triangular shell, from the front of which extended a long neck. Out of this neck bulged two beady little eyes. From both sides of the shell, or carapace, shot long, spindly legs, giving the crustacean a total width of about two inches. The neck crab was what is known as a decorator crab, his legs overgrown with tiny flowerlike hydroids. He looked like a fuzzy bowtie.

Henry was incredulous. "Now *why* would I want to decorate a fish whose favorite meal is *crab?*"

"But it's a special occasion. You would add such a nice touch. Just dangle from his neck—stay under his chin away from his mouth. Don't pull any tricks. He won't even know you're there," said the hogfish, smoothly.

The crab considered this. He was known as a decorator crab because he adorned himself with tiny flowerlike hydroids in order to hide from predators. That others considered him as a decoration was a new concept to Henry. The neck crab scratched his neck with a claw-foot.

Hmmm, I could actually have some fun with this, he thought to himself. Then he said aloud, "But what about his gal? She'll go right for me when she nuzzles his neck."

"So you can jump ship if things get out of hand," insisted the hogfish.

Henry thought some more. "Well, okay. But if he starts getting rowdy I'm gonna pinch him and climb inside his gills and make his life miserable."

The tiny Spanish hogfish gently took the tiny crab by a leg with his mouth and carried him to Cooper's chin. The crab reached out with a clawfoot and grabbed onto a gill cover. He gave Cooper a test pinch.

"Ouch! Whoa. Hey, what was that!" Cooper's fins sprang out, as he snapped out of his trance.

Then the neck crab tickled Cooper under the chin. "Cootchie cootchie coo!" he teased.

A Spunky Grouper

"Hoo hoo hoo!" giggled Cooper. "I don't know what that was, but it sure felt good!"

Ah! Decent. This guy is under control, thought the crab. He felt better about his new job as a fish ornament.

The grouper felt like a new fish. In fact, he glowed. "Hey, guys—today started all wrong. My bones felt so funky. But with much thanks to you, I now feel quite spunky!"

Cooper bowed to his friends. The cleaners all cheered and wished him well. Henry waved his legs. And with great aplomb, Cooper the Grouper swaggered off toward Sadie's, wagging his tail behind him all the way.

Sadie's neighborhood was in a network of tiny patch reefs. They resembled a complex of whimsical apartment buildings overgrown with sponges and soft corals. Paths of sand wove around and through the coral patches, looking like the winding streets of a quaint village. Sea plumes growing from bare spots on coral heads swayed with the gentle current.

Sadie's den was under a giant mound of star coral that looked like a Japanese pagoda. Outside the entrance was a courtyard of sorts, over which hung branches of more sea plumes. A fat conch shell inhabited by a tiny juvenile spotted drum lay in the sand outside Sadie's door. The exotic-looking black and white fish started swimming wildly in tiny figure eights when the grouper approached his domain.

Cooper settled quietly in the sand outside Sadie's door. A tiny secretary blenny poked its head out of an old worm tube above Sadie's den, and took note of the visitor.

The spunky grouper hesitated.

"What if she doesn't want me around?" He became gloomy again. Then he pulled himself together. With all the nerve he could muster up, he cleared his throat.

"Sadie?" he called softly, with a gravelly voice.

There was no answer. He waited.

"Saaay-deee..."

Again, there was no answer.

Maybe she's just out for a bite to eat, he thought.

Cooper settled on his tail and waited some more. He waited, and waited. And waited some more.

But Sadie just didn't come back.

Cooper now felt lonelier and more miserable than ever. He worried about Sadie. He sat in the sand at Sadie's door, absently watching two courting jawfish. They darted around and around each other just above their holes in the sand bottom.

"Hmmph! You'd think they could wait for the moon to get full!" he muttered to himself. Cooper moved to a different spot and brooded some more.

"Things are not right," said he. "Something's amiss. I'm not accustomed to feeling like this... I'm feeling odd. I'm lonely and grumpy. I'm hungry, I'm rest-less—and feeling quite jumpy.

"Could it be love? Now, there's no way to know. And here I am, all cleaned up, and there's no place to go."

Waiting for Sadie

"Aw, come on, *give* me a *break!*" came a high-pitched, raspy voice to Cooper's ear.

"Huh?" the grouper hadn't realized that he had company. "What and where are you?" Cooper demanded. His eyes rotated, unable to find the source.

"I'll never tell! But I am here to spiff you up," answered the crustacean, giving the big fish a poke with his claw.

"Ouch! Hmmph. All you're doing is making me crabby," sulked the grouper.

"More than you'll ever know," said Henry the neck crab, giving Cooper a pinch.

"Ouch!" snapped the grouper again.

Cooper was depressed. And as the afternoon progressed, the grouper's anxiety increased. He didn't feel like going home to his grotto. Nor did he feel like going to any of his favorite hangouts. He started wandering aimlessly, not paying attention to where he was going. He just didn't care anymore. He was lost in himself—or outside of himself. He didn't know which.

But the grouper's anxiety and depression waned and was gradually replaced by a new feeling. A feeling of being pulled by some kind of force. When he finally became aware of this strange new feeling, he didn't know what to make of it—any more than he understood anything else that was happening to him.

"It fills me inside from my tail to my face. I feel in my bones that there's some far-off place calling me. But to where? To where? That, I cannot explain. But in this place, I know that I cannot remain.

"My brain says 'Stay, stay', and my heart says, 'No, no!' Whoa, it's a hard choice to make, 'cause my bones say, 'Go, *go!*'"

And with that, Cooper knew he must be gone.

He didn't understand it, but he followed the feeling in his bones as he hurried to the drop-off. When he reached it, he swam out from the reef wall. When the current felt right against his face, he was off.

To where, he knew not. He followed the reef wall along the island of Macquerupa, heading east. There was an urgency that he didn't understand, but it didn't seem to matter now. He just gave in to his bones. They told him where to go—and that something very important was at stake.

CHAPTER IX

The Old Neighborhood

MARGARET Thomas and her sister, Opal Brown, visited over cocoa tea on the front porch. Opal liked drinking hot drinks on hot days. She thought if she could raise her body temperature, the air wouldn't seem as hot as it actually was. The two women fanned themselves with folded newspapers.

"Renny just hasn't seemed like himself lately," said Margaret, her eyes watching the water below.

"Well, he is at the age now where boys and girls go through changes," said Opal, with authority. Opal was twenty years older than Margaret.

"Yes, but this seems different," said Margaret. "He's still very polite. He doesn't talk back, and he does do what he is told to do. But he does seem very preoccupied."

"Oh? Well, he is at the age where boys and girls have many things on their minds," replied Opal.

"I don't know," continued Margaret. "He just doesn't seem right. It seems almost like he is hidin' somethin'. He never has done that before."

"Oh? Well, this is the age where boys and girls start hidin' things," said Opal.

Margaret glared at her older sister. "What do *you* know?" she said.

Opal winced. "Well, I was not born yesterday. I have learned a few things in my time. So tell me how Renny is any different than any other boy his age."

"Well, for one thing, J.D. wants to teach Renny to scuba dive, and now Renny does not want to learn. Renny *always* has wanted to learn to scuba dive! I don't understand it. He always goes to the cove, but he does not tell about what he sees there anymore. He always has been full of stories about what he sees out there. And those new fins—" Mrs. Thomas' eyes widened. "Why, it is almost as if this all started on Christmas, with those new fins!"

"Oh? Fins? Now tell me why new fins should change a boy," said Opal. "Maybe he is sweet on the little McKenna girl."

Just then, the two ladies were distracted by the rustling of leaves from across the yard.

"Hey, Auntie Opal! Hi, Mom!" called Renny from across the yard. He emerged from the jungle through the clump of banana trees, and hurried past the women on the porch. The screen door slammed behind him as he went inside.

Opal and Margaret looked at the door, and then looked at each other.

"He seems perfectly normal to me," said Opal, raising her eyebrows.

Renny had been down at the cove with J.D., who

had been telling Renny about his plans for the dive resort. He had been showing Renny around the property, talking about his life as a Navy kid thirty years before.

"I was about eight when we moved here and about your age when we left. Come on, I'll show you where we lived."

J.D. and Renny crawled through a rip in the old chain-link fence that separated his property from the rest of the old Navy neighborhood. A weathered sign dangling nearby on the fence said,

KEEP OUT

They walked past the tennis court remains, down the old street. Some of the houses were currently occupied by locals, were kept up, and had neatly trimmed yards. The rest were empty, with torn window screens, rotted wooden shutters, and yards that were being reclaimed by the jungle. Most of the concrete houses stood on square concrete columns.

"Why are the houses on stilts?" asked Renny.

"To catch the breeze and keep out the water during the rainy season. Yours is on the hillside and already catches the breeze. Being on stilts also helps keep out the vermin—except of course for baby alligators. They used to get in the sewer and come up into people's toilets."

"Aw, you're pullin' my leg," said Renny.

"It's true! My mom flushed one back down the toilet one time, and the next morning she heard this piercing scream from the next house. It was Mrs.

Larson. Later that morning at the club, Mrs. Larson says, 'Guess what I found in *my* toilet this morning!' And my mom says all sweet and innocent-like, 'A little 'ole alligator?' Mrs. Larson didn't like my mom ruining her story," J.D. said.

"Yeah," said Renny. "Sounds like Auntie Opal."

"Sometimes we would go on *big* alligator hunts in the jungle, up the dry creek beds. Do you ever do that?" asked J.D..

"Nah. Never have," said Renny. "My mom would have a fit."

"Yeah, my mom sure did," J.D. said. "Except that we kids always had a gardener with us who carried a big machete. We were thankful for gardeners with machetes—and for snack bar attendants on the beach. They were our guardian angels. We would get in the craziest binds. Our moms were always off playing cards, leaving us to run wild—at least we thought so, anyway. We had the greatest time exploring the jungle and never thought anything of it.

"Until one day, when my dad showed me a big, dead bushmaster... He hung it on that big 'ole tree, right over there," said J.D., pointing down the street. "That snake scared the daylights out of me—for about a week, anyway. Then I was back out messing around in the jungle again. But a gardener with his machete always seemed to appear out of nowhere when things got interesting."

J.D. stopped in front of a house whose overgrown yard was lined with royal palms, bougainvilla and hibiscus bushes. "These were the Admiral's quarters. We used to ride our bikes through his garden. It had a winding path that was a lot more fun than the street was. His wife never yelled at us, even once."

"Maybe she was always at the clubhouse playin' cards while you were in her yard," quipped Renny.

"Ha! Maybe so," said J.D..

They continued down another street, past more concrete houses on stilts. Then J.D. stopped again.

"Here it is," he said. "My old house. It looks pretty good after all these years."

"Hey, my friend Matty lives here!" said Renny. "He could give you a tour if you wanted."

J.D. was thoughtful for a moment.

"No thanks. I think I'd like to remember my house as my house, not someone else's," J.D. said quietly.

With their hands in their pockets, the two of them stood on the street looking at J.D.'s old house.

"Some things you just can't go back to. Some things you can restore, some things you can't. You can restore buildings, but you can't restore living things, once they're gone," said J.D..

They were quiet for a few more minutes.

"J.D., I'm afraid for my reef. I don't want it getting wrecked and over-dived like other reefs," blurted Renny.

J.D. looked at Renny in surprise. "So that's why you don't like my plans, eh?"

"Yeah, I guess so," said the boy, looking down. He swung his foot back and forth across the gravel.

"You know, Renny, I love that reef as much as you do. I don't want anything to happen to it any more than you do," said J.D..

"So why can't we just keep it to ourselves?" asked Renny, looking up at J.D. with hope.

J.D. sighed. "Hmmm. Well, that's a tough one. Some things you can keep to yourself. And some things you just can't. A reef like ours is too good to keep a secret. Plus, it's not really ours, anyway. The world's going to find out about it sooner or later. That property was for sale. It was advertised all over. Now aren't you glad someone who loves it as you do jumped on it, rather than some outfit just out for the bucks?"

"Yeah, I guess," said Renny.

"Well, this is our chance to take the reins and do it the way we want to do it. If someone else had bought the property, you never know what would happen to it. Sometimes you can't just sit back and wait for stuff to happen. You have to get in there yourself if you want a say-so in things. It might mean sticking out your neck a bit, taking a few risks, or having to compromise, but that's what the world is

all about, Renny. It's a big world out there, and this
island—like it or not—is part of it."

"But how can we keep our reef from gettin' over-
dived? And what about the bulldozers? And the dirt
runnin' into the sea? I saw where the water was turnin' orange when it rained. It'll kill the reef!"

J.D. looked at Renny with concern.

"You're right," he said. "But I don't want to rush
into anything. I want to do it right. It isn't going to
be a big fancy place. And there's a lot I need to learn
before I go diving into a project like this. But I'll
keep an open mind and make sure I don't do anything to mess up our reef," said J.D..

Renny was thoughtful for a few minutes.

"J.D.?" Renny said.

"Yeah."

"Would you really teach me how to scuba dive?"

"Hey, you bet!" said J.D..

"But equipment costs so much money," said Renny.

"Well, you'd have to work for it. And I would want
you to be a dive guide for my guests," said J.D., looking at Renny.

Renny was quiet. He still wasn't sure he wanted
to share his reef with strangers. Would they want to
spearfish? Would they discover the grotto? Would
they find his grouper? But wait—if *he* was the dive
guide, maybe he could keep other divers away from
the grotto and the grouper. Maybe he could have
some say-so over where on the reef they could go.

"J.D.?" Renny said.

"Yeah."

"If I learn to scuba dive and be a dive guide for your tourists, would I have to share everythin' about my reef?" asked Renny.

J.D. cocked his head and looked at the boy thoughtfully. "As I said, some things you share. And some things are for keeping to yourself. How come?"

Renny had an idea he wasn't ready to share.

"Oh, I doh know...hey, J.D.! I jus' remembered somethin' I hafta do. I hafta go now. See yuh later!"

Renny turned and sprinted off toward his house, leaving his friend in the street. J.D. just stood there, shaking his head.

Just when I thought I was beginning to understand kids, he thought.

"I'm goin' out to the reef now! Bye, Mom! Bye, Auntie!" Renny zoomed off with his snorkeling gear, disappearing behind the clump of banana trees as quickly as he had appeared just seconds before, leaving behind two puzzled ladies.

"You be careful, hear? And stay away from the drop-off! And quit slammin' the door!" Margaret called to Renny.

Margaret and Opal looked at each other and shook their heads.

"Kids," they said in unison.

CHAPTER X

Becoming Enlightened

RENNY ran for the cove, arrived at the beach, donned his gear and sped out to the drop-off. He had a mission. It didn't matter that he wasn't supposed to go out there. He had to know if his grotto experience on Christmas afternoon was for real. He was full of questions and had decided it was time for answers.

Did I really not have to breathe when I was in the grotto? Was I really talking with the grouper—or was everything just in my head? Was it all a crazy dream? If I go back, will the same thing happen again? Is this a magic place where I can have gills?

If I don't have to breathe when I'm there, why would I even *need* to learn to scuba dive? This place could be my hideout! It's the best place on the reef— I wouldn't have to go anywhere else. If I can talk to the grouper, can I talk to other fishes, too?

Wow, that would really be something. To have gills and be able to talk to fishes. I wouldn't have to share my reef with tourists at all. I could just go to the grotto and be happy—but then J.D. would get someone else to be a dive guide—and they might find the grotto. What if someone followed me?

But *man!* The drop-off is forbidden. How could I go out there without getting caught? Wow, if Mom and Dad ever found out—what if they missed me and couldn't find me and thought I had drowned? What if they had heart attacks and I was the cause?

Will the grouper still be there? Will he be going to Grouper Moon? What if he gets caught? If he hasn't left yet, maybe I could warn him not to go. Maybe I could save his life! If I could do that, then I wouldn't care about getting in trouble. It would be worth it...

All kinds of thoughts raced through Renny's mind as he kicked hard. He found his reef markers, found the big "G," and headed out, using the sand channel below to guide him. It cut deeper in the coral to become the familiar sand chute. When it came to an end, Renny took a deep breath and went down. There it was, the big clump of tube sponges where the chute stopped. The boy carefully slid through the sea plumes to the opening of the grotto.

Renny hadn't remembered the opening to the grotto being so narrow. He could barely get through it. But sure enough, when he entered, there it all was. That great sense of peace and security was back. The shimmering silversides were still there, and were just as beautiful. He glided in and lay down in the sand bottom on his back, with his hands behind his head. He watched the passing sea life through the lace-fringed openings above.

It was true. He didn't need to breathe when he was in this place. But, wanting to be sure, he went back outside to the sand channel again. He had to return to the surface for air. He went down again, back into the grotto and waited. He didn't need to breathe. It was amazing. He continued on through the cavern, through the mass of silversides who parted around him. This is so wild! thought Renny.

He felt something soft and silky gently sliding across his arm.

"You're back." It was the green moray.

"Yeah, I had to come again. I had to see if this place was for real." Renny reached for the moray and tentatively touched it. "It sure feels safe in here."

"Oh, yes, it is safe all right. It is very safe. Nice and dark, too. Yes, you could stay here and be very safe indeed." The moray circled Renny and faced him.

Renny began to stroke the moray. He loved the feel of its skin. "Do you ever leave this grotto?"

"Why should I ever want to leave this place when everything I need is right here?" The eel brushed against Renny again. It liked to be stroked. Renny's skin felt good.

"But don't you ever want to get out where it's light?" Renny wondered.

The moray went back into a crack and stuck out his head. "Why should I ever need to do that? I'm a creature of the dark. And I'm safe here. I can view the outside world from the safety of my cave through many windows. I need not make myself vulnerable to the outside. My food wanders in through the dark. I can chase it through dark tunnels and crannies. I need nothing else. I'm quite content." The moray looked at Renny with his deep-violet eyes.

"Well, don't you grow tired of being in the dark

all the time? It is, after all, a very beautiful reef out there." Renny shifted and moved toward the opening to the wall. He wanted to see the beautiful view of the drop-off again.

And there it was, in all its splendor, right before his eyes—the grand parade of creole wrasse, the angelfish, and huge sponges. The black forest of immense gorgonians hanging from the wall, the sea plumes at the top. The barrel was still there, too. But there was no grouper sitting on it, taking in the view.

Renny lay down on his belly next to the barrel, just as he had done before, to gaze at the world before him. The creole wrasse parade went past again—and again and again. The angelfish passed by, back and forth. The sea plumes wafted back and forth, back and forth in the gentle current. Life passed by, back and forth. Renny became hypnotized by it all.

"See?" the eel slinked up next to Renny. "It's all right here. All you need. Isn't it wonderful?"

"Yeah, it sure is." But something in Renny was starting to nag at him, as the scene kept repeating itself, back and forth. "But have you seen what else is out there, beyond this awesome view?" Renny looked at the moray.

"Why should I need to, when I am satisfied with things just the way they are?" The moray brushed up against Renny again.

Renny's mind shifted. "Have you seen the Nassau grouper?"

"Oh, you mean Cooper?" The eel squirmed.

"He has a name?" Renny's eyes widened.

"Yeah, why wouldn't he? My name is Maurice, by the way. No, I haven't seen him all afternoon. He started getting all wound up this morning, and then he just left. A bunch of his kind stopped by a while ago, looking for him. Said there was a bash going on." Maurice swam out of the opening and came back again.

"Friends? A bash? You mean there were other Nassaus?" Renny's head tilted to the side.

"Yeah, yeah, a whole big gang of 'em. Said they were trying to round everyone up, but they couldn't find Coop."

"Wow," Renny thought. He wondered what it would be like to see a big school of Nassau grouper.

Maurice the moray continued, "I can't imagine what possessed the poor guy. He's a loner, like me— except, of course, that we're huntin' buddies. But Coop, he just started going nuts all of a sudden. I told him to go get cleaned up or somethin' so he'd feel better. So he did. But then he never came back.

And here I was planning to flush him out a nice perfect little crab tonight—just the way he likes 'em. Big ones give him the worst bellyaches."

"Did his friends say where this bash was going to be?" Renny giggled to himself at the thought of an eel trying to make a grouper feel better.

"Hey, what's so funny about that?" The moray brushed against Renny again. "Yeah, they said if anyone saw Coop, to tell him to meet 'em up at the end of the island, up that-a-way." Maurice swam out over the drop-off again, and wiggled his head toward the east. "They said it was very important, that all the Nassaus needed him there."

Renny grew concerned. "It's Grouper Moon." Renny shifted.

"Grouper *what?*"

"Grouper Moon. That's when they all get together and do their roein'. And all the fishermen from all over the island are going to be there waiting for them. I wanted to warn the grouper."

"Dang. See what I mean? You're safe as long as you stay in the dark. As soon as you leave, BAM! You're exposed and vulnerable." The moray started snaking back and forth.

Renny was quiet for a few minutes.

"Well, I guess if he just stayed in his cave, and so did all the other Nassaus in their own safe little dens, they would live for long time. But what kind of life would that be?"

"Who cares? It's fine right here."

"But there's a big reef out there! Plus, they'd never get to see each other and have their young. So what would happen to their kind?" Renny glided toward Maurice.

"Why should it matter?" The moray circled Renny.

"Don't you feel at all responsible for what happens to *your* kind?" Renny moved back to the opening and gazed at the parade of creole wrasse.

"Hmmm. Can't say I've given it much thought." Maurice slinked past Renny again.

"What would the reef be like without any green morays?" Renny held his arms out and brought his hands together, forming a ring.

"Don't know that it would make much difference one way or another. Who knows? It might even be a better place." Maurice slithered through the ring that Renny made with his arms.

"Yeah, but what if all the other creatures of the world felt that way, and didn't care?" Renny took down his arms and sat down by the barrel.

The eel settled in the grouper's spot on the barrel next to Renny, and gazed out beyond the wall. He was quiet for a few minutes. Then he turned his face toward Renny.

"Hmmm. So our Cooper has been pulled out of his safe little world for a higher cause, even if it means risking his tail. No wonder he was going bonkers. Poor guy." Maurice laid his head down in the sand.

Renny was silent while he thought about that. Then up shot his eyebrows.

CHAPTER XI

The Corrida

NIGHT fell, and Cooper could see the big white moon in the sky. Its light guided him along the edge of the reef wall. Although he had no idea what it was, Cooper knew he was on an important mission. He continued swimming all night long, his body wagging all the way. When daybreak came, he didn't even notice the changeover on the reef.

He was now in deep water. Any creatures that had been out had quickly taken cover at the appearance of a strange big fish. The reef looked empty, and Cooper was all alone, but he didn't notice. He just doggedly followed the reef wall and the feeling in his bones.

An enormous formation in the shape of an arch appeared before him. It was covered with brownish sponges in freeform shapes, and laced with the giant black gorgonians so common to the wall. Corals at this depth looked like thin saucers sticking out of the wall. Intrigued, Cooper stopped to poke around the structure. Coral architecture fascinated him. Shaped by the individual growth patterns of coral and by water currents, the arch was truly Nature's design. Cooper thought it was quite beautiful.

There was a fleeting feeling that he had been in this place before, but Cooper couldn't imagine when that would have been. How much of his younger life could he remember? He wasn't sure. He became lost in thought as he pondered these things.

Suddenly, Cooper's body sensed a presence nearby. His fins shot out with alarm as he dove for cover behind the arch. When he felt safe enough, he turned back to peep through the sponges. A huge shape loomed in the distance. He watched as the shape moved toward him through the water. When it got close enough, he could see that it was not one big shape at all, but that it was a school of fish. He cocked his left eye. Then he cocked his right eye. This was something new. He cocked both eyes together. He couldn't believe what they were seeing.

"Whoa. Oh *my!*" he said softly, in his hoarse voice.

It was a group of fish. A group of groupers. A group of Nassau groupers. A group of Nassau groupers of many sizes. Cooper cautiously emerged from his hiding place. The group was passing by without even noticing him.

"Hey," Cooper shyly called to the group.

The group stopped, and all the fish turned in unison to look at him. Then one of them spoke up.

"Hey, group! It's Coop!"

Cooper's eyes popped.

"Louie? Is that *you?*"

"Yeah, Coop, it's me! Hey, get your tail over here! We were wondering where you were. We were trying to round you up, but didn't see you when we passed by your place. Neither had any of the other guys around your parts. Your huntin' buddy was kind of worried about you."

"Whoa, I've been worried, too. Feeling so funny and restless," Cooper replied, "And lonely. It's so odd.

I'm a grouper—I'm not supposed to feel lonely—or jumpy, or cranky, for that matter. It's just not like me. I don't know what's going on. All I know is that my bones are telling me to go somewhere. So I'm going. But I have no idea where! I don't understand it one bit. And now I run into a group of groupers. Groupers don't do groups! What *is* this all about!?"

The group looked at Cooper, incredulously.

"You don't *know?*" chorused the group.

"Well, what do you all expect?" said Louie, turning toward the groupers. "Don't you remember *your* first few times?"

"I remember mine," volunteered one. "My first one or two took me totally by surprise. But after a few more of these journeys, you start to recognize the signs—like feeling restless and lonely. Then you know it's time to go again."

"But time to go *where?*" Cooper wanted to know.

"To the end of our island—the end of our world! It's Grouper Moon!" chorused the group, impatiently.

"Grouper *what?*"

Then the biggest Nassau grouper that Cooper had ever seen in his entire seven years of life swam forward.

"I'm Uncle Epinephelus," he said, in a deep, rich and friendly voice. He waved his pectoral fins politely.

"Epi-*who?*"

"Ep - ee - NEF - uh - luss," Uncle Epinephelus said, patiently. "It's our family name. I get to use it because I am an elder."

"A what?" said Cooper.

"An elder. A great, wise grouper. The eldest of our aggregation. The greatest and wisest grouper in this group. I've been through this journey many times. Let me explain:

"It happens one time every year, so we're told— when the water feels right—not too warm, not too cold. And the moon's waxing full—not too new, not too old. The great gathering of Nassaus—a sight to behold!"

Another grouper sashayed forward. "I'm Greg, and well known for my *great* cerebration. This party— this bash—it's a *great* celebration! We Nassaus are loners, with just one convocation each year—when we gather as one *great* grouper nation!"

"Whoa. Just to party?" Cooper asked.

"There's more to it than that," Epinephelus said. "We Nassaus are loners, but our genes must be spread. In this great aggregation, our gametes are shed. If it weren't for our party, our kind would be dead.

"So Nature's arranged for our dance. Once a year, Nassaus from all over the island appear—at a prearranged place, not too far from here. But the moon must be full, and the sky must be clear.

"The full moon at sunset is when we must dance. So we all must be there, or we'll forfeit our chance. Now, let's hurry along, or we won't get to prance. We'll miss the whole party, and will have *no* romance."

With that, the group all turned away from Cooper, and started moving again along the reef face. So Cooper joined the big group of his own kind, known to islanders as a *corrida*—a school of Nassau grouper on the way to their spawning grounds.

For the first time since yelling at the parrotfish, Cooper felt as if things were actually starting to make sense. He wasn't all cleaned up for nothing. There really was a place to go. It was time to spawn. With this knowledge, Cooper felt more grown-up, and held his head a little higher.

"By the way, Coop, nice tie," Louie said.

"Huh?" Cooper said.

"He said, 'nice tie'!" Cooper heard that thin, raspy voice in his ear again, accompanied by a pinch in his gill flap.

"Hey!" yelped Cooper.

"Here I am, sticking out my neck, just to make you

look spiffy. I hope you appreciate it," muttered the neck crab under his breath.

Cooper swam next to Louie, who pointed out various distinctive reef structures. These would be good landmarks for finding his way back home, and for finding his way back to Rocky Point in future years. Along the way, they picked up more Nassau groupers, some of whom were traveling solo, and some who were already in small groups.

With his body on autopilot, Cooper had plenty of time to think along the way. He wondered what the party would be like. His new friends said there would be thousands of Nassaus there. He couldn't even imagine so many groupers together in one place. Would Sadie be there? Is that why she wasn't home?

He wondered why groupers were solitary sorts during the rest of the year. Why was there just one dance a year? Was the party that bad? Did they see so much of each other during the party that they didn't want to see each other for the rest of the year? Or was it so good that the experience was enough to last for a whole year?

Why did they all have to meet in this far-off place to spawn? Why couldn't he and Sadie just pair up on their own part of the reef and have their young and take care of them—as do the sergeant majors— or the hamlets, who danced every day at sunset during the evening changeover?

What would happen to all the new grouper eggs? Where would they go? Would he ever get to see any of his young? He sighed. It was hard understanding Nature's way.

It was starting to get dark. Finally, the grouper corrida slowed. Cooper noticed that the reef face had ended. There was a change in current. Was it was the end of the reef? No, wait—not the end, but just where the reef face took a very sharp turn and angled back the other way. It was a point at the northeast corner of the island.

Cooper heard mumbling among the other Nassau groupers. Where was the party? The group stopped, and went deeper, to a flatter part of the reef under the jutting promontory. There they found others milling around. Cooper had never seen so many Nassau groupers! But something wasn't right. He sensed worry among them.

Cooper grew concerned. He thought parties were supposed to be fun. But he was too exhausted to give any more thought to it all. He found a ledge and joined several other groupers who had just settled in, also tired from their long journeys.

Cooper slept and dreamed of Sadie. He dreamed of the two of them on their own reef, paired. They were proud parents of lots of little Nassau groupers, who followed them around the reef...

"Come, come, little groupies! Come along, now," said Cooper, in his sleep.

CHAPTER XII

Beryl

THE pleasant-looking woman at the table was looking through binoculars. Margaret Thomas squinted her eyes, and tried to see what the woman saw. But Margaret couldn't see the frigatebird catch a tropicbird by the tail in mid-air in an attempt to force the tropicbird to drop its fish.

"Whoa!" exclaimed the woman as she watched the air show.

"Nice view, eh?" Margaret said to the woman.

"Boy, I'll say!" replied the woman, setting down her binoculars on the table. She looked up at Mrs.

Thomas with bright, clear eyes. "It sure is gorgeous out there."

Mrs. Thomas beamed. "It is our heaven on Earth. What can I get for you?"

"What are you cooking tonight?"

"Snapper and kingfish."

"Snapper sounds good," said the woman. Her rich, mellow voice had a familiar British lilt to it. She was slim, with skin the color of coffee, and had long, frizzy black hair tied back in a ponytail. She wore navy blue Bermuda shorts and a short-sleeved white blouse with a name badge pinned to it. The badge identified her as Beryl Piscado, a biologist with the Department of the Environment.

"Coming right up," replied Margaret. She disappeared into the kitchen. The sound of clanking dishes could be heard through the window.

Margaret put a pan of water on the stove to boil, and sat down to wait for it. Then she grated a cocoa ball into the pan of boiling water. She threw in some sugar and a bay leaf and poured milk into the mixture. Pouring some into a cup, she returned the pan to the stove, and took the cup out to the woman.

"Would you like some cocoa tea? I just made some," said Margaret, as she set down the cup in front of Beryl.

"Sure, thank you," replied Beryl, seeing that she really had no choice about it.

There was an old cocoa plantation nearby, growing up the mountainside. It had been hard working the plantation, which was too steep for modern machinery. The pods had to be harvested by hand.

Workers had to cut them from the trees, then roll them down the mountainside to be collected.

The workers eventually left the plantation to fish. They could make more money with less effort. The plantation went out of business, left to the locals to harvest the cocoa pods for themselves. They would process the seeds and pulp inside the pods and shape the product into balls resembling small, dark brown potatoes. This was pure, unadulterated chocolate—used for cooking and making cocoa tea. It could last for months or even years on the shelf.

Margaret returned to the kitchen, and could be heard banging more pots and pans as she started dinner.

What a noisy cook, thought Beryl, amused, as she sipped her cocoa tea. It tasted rich and delicious.

Picking up her binoculars again, she looked for the frigatebird, only to be distracted again—this time by the rustling of leaves across the yard. Renny emerged through the clump of banana trees and walked toward the front porch. His mask and snorkel sat atop his forehead, and his fins hung from his shoulder. He was wearing his new socks, stained orange from the dirt. He stopped when he saw Beryl at the table. She was looking at Renny with interest.

"Hello there," she said, cheerfully.

"Hello," replied Renny, politely reserved.

"See anything interesting out there?"

Renny was just returning from his encounter with the moray eel in the grotto at the drop-off.

"Nah," he said, looking down.

Mrs. Thomas walked out from the kitchen with

silverware and a glass of water. "Hello Renny," she said. Turning to the woman, she added, "He's not bothering you, is he?"

"Of course not! I'm having a very interesting conversation with this young man. Is he your son?"

"This is Renny. He is my boy," beamed Mrs. Thomas. "And I am his mother, Margaret."

The woman stuck out her hand. "I'm Beryl."

"What kind of biologist are you?" asked Renny, looking at her name badge.

"A fish biologist. I'm here to study the Nassau grouper catch when it starts coming in," replied Beryl.

"You are?"

"Yes, we're studying the Nassaus. They're ordinarily hard to study, because they're solitary fish. So when the catch comes in, we like to be there so we can use the fish that are already caught to do some of our studies."

"Why are you studying the Nassaus?"

"Because they're very important fish."

"They are?"

"Both on the reef and to man. They're important on the reef because they're one of the top predators. They're important to man because they are very tasty."

"My mom makes the best grouper on the island," Renny said proudly, looking up at his mother.

"Yes ma'am, I do," said Margaret.

"That's what I've heard," Beryl replied, warmly. The smell of bread baking in the oven filled the air.

"I'll go see about your dinner now," said Margaret.

"What kinds of studies do you do on the Nassaus?" Renny asked Beryl. He sat down at the table.

"We count them to see how many were taken—total and per boat—and measure them and weigh them. We identify them as males or females, see if they've still got eggs and milt in them—that sort of thing," Beryl said.

"What's milt?" asked Renny.

"Milt is the sperm from the males that fertilizes the eggs from the females," said Beryl.

"Oh. Why do you want to see if they still have eggs and stuff?" said Renny.

"Well, if the females still have eggs inside, that means they've gotten caught before they've had a chance to spawn," Beryl said.

"My dad says they're easy to catch when they're roein'," said Renny. "That's the same thing as spawnin', right?"

"Yes," Beryl smiled. "They call fish eggs "roe". So your dad means when the females are shedding their eggs. But actually, most of the fish aggregate a couple of days before they shed their eggs—to mill around, do their courting, and wait for everyone to get there. Then they all spawn together at sunset just after the full moon," said Beryl. "So it's actually during the few days *before* they spawn that most of them are caught."

"What does aggregate mean?"

"It means 'to gather together.' An aggregation of fish is a school of fish, but in this case of the groupers, an aggregation is an incredibly big school of fish. These fish have come from all over the island

and from great distances to aggregate," said Beryl.

"Why do they aggregate to spawn?" Renny asked.

"That's a good question," said Beryl. "But first, tell me what you know about Nassaus."

"Well, I know they like to be alone," said Renny. "But I always wondered why they're called groupers if they don't like to be in groups. Seems like a funny name for a fish who's a loner."

The biologist grinned. "Yes, it is strange that loners should be called groupers. Actually, we believe the name 'grouper' comes from the word garrupa. It's Portuguese, probably after a South American Indian name for the groupers," said Beryl.

"So why do they spawn only once a year?" said Renny.

"Well, it seems that fish who are loners just don't get to see each other often enough. There aren't as many groupers around as there are other kinds of fish, and besides, they're spread out all over the reef."

"How come?"

"Well, generally the larger the animal, the closer to the top of the food chain it is. Groupers are one of the top predators on the reef. The reef can have no more than a few top predators.

"Groupers are also very slow growing and live a long time, so they don't have to reproduce as often as smaller, more short-lived species. But when the groupers do spawn, Mother Nature has them make the best use of the opportunity," said Beryl.

"So why do they go to Rocky Point to spawn?" asked Renny.

"Many of the aggregations in the Caribbean seem

to happen off the easternmost or northeasternmost points of land masses. We think it's because the currents at those places are better for carrying off the spawn—and even perhaps for later returning them to the shallows."

Margaret appeared from the kitchen, carrying a bowl of steaming soup. "Would you like some callaloo?" she said as she set down the bowl before Beryl.

"It smells great! Is it made with meat or seafood?" asked Beryl.

"I made it with crab," said Margaret. "It is the best on the island."

"I'm sure it is," smiled Beryl. "I never have been able to make a good callaloo."

"Oh, it is very easy. Just some dasheen leaves boiled in a broth with okroes and pumpkin and this and that—whatever I have on hand," said Margaret— not adding that she flavored it with pig tail and co- conut.

"Maybe Renny would like some, too," said Beryl. "I hate eating in front of anyone."

Renny looked up at his mother with interest.

"Would you like some, too, Renny?" said his mother.

"Sure. I'll come and get it myself," he said, getting up from the table.

"So why do Nassaus spawn in January and not at other times?" asked Renny, as he returned to the table with his soup.

"Actually, in some places, Grouper Moon has been known to happen in December and February, as well as January. Around Macquerupa, Grouper Moon can be in December or January, depending on when the full moon is. Why they gather during that time of year may be related to the water temperature. In some places they spawn later. In Bermuda, way north of here where it takes longer for the water temperature to warm up, Grouper Moon may not happen until summer." said Beryl.

Renny's interest grew. "Does Grouper Moon always happen around the time of a full moon?" he asked.

"Yes," Beryl said.

"Why?"

"Well, tidal currents are stronger during new and full moons. So spawning on the full moon would increase the likelihood that outgoing currents on the ebb tide would be stronger—better for carrying away the spawn," said Beryl.

"Why is it good for the spawn to be carried away from the reef?" asked Renny.

"Fish eggs drift as part of the plankton. They are totally helpless. Since there are more predators on the reef than there are in the open water, being away from the reef gives them a better chance of survival during their early lives," said Beryl.

"You said before that the groupers spawn at sunset. Why do they wait until sunset?" asked Renny.

"Spawning at sunset is an advantage because it's the changeover period, and during this time neither the day-active nor the night-active fish can see as well. So the eggs are not as visible then. Many species of reef fish spawn at this time."

"Wow. So the fish spawn at sunset, and the currents carry the eggs off into the dark. It's like a great escape!" said Renny.

"Exactly," grinned Beryl.

"But how do they get back to the reef?" asked Renny.

"Probably currents. Sometimes storms will wash them into the shallows. Or they may get carried to some other far-off place. And there is evidence that they may even get back to the shallows on their own, although it's hard to imagine how."

"How long do they stay out in the ocean before they come back to the reef to live?"

"Anywhere from 35 to 50 days. But before they actually move to the reef, they start out their new lives in the turtle grass beds. "

"I've never noticed any baby fish in the turtle grass," said Renny.

"You have to get down and look very closely. They're teensy, and very cryptic—hard to see. But they are there. All kinds of baby fishes hang out there. In fact, that's why they call the turtle grass beds the nurseries of the reef," said Beryl.

"Wow," said Renny. "I've never seen babies in the turtle grass. But I do see lots of young fish around patch reefs and coral clumps in the sand."

"That's because the patch reefs are where the young go to after they get big enough to leave the turtle grass nurseries. Sort of like graduating to kindergarten," said Beryl. "Then as they get even bigger, they'll move onto the reef itself. Then they move to even deeper water. We see the really big ones at the drop-offs."

Margaret appeared again with dinner for both Beryl and Renny.

"Here you go, fresh snapper, catch of the day. I made some coo-coo to go with it. I hope you like coo-coo. And some hops bread." Coo-coo was a corn-meal and okra side dish.

"Mmmm," said Beryl. "Thanks. It all looks delicious. I've been having quite a conversation with Renny. He is very bright."

Margaret beamed, "He's a smart one all right. We hope he can get a good education and make something of himself. We have high hopes for our boy."

Renny blushed. "Aw, she's always full of ol' talk."

Margaret and Beryl laughed.

"But I can see that you're going to have no trouble at all in the brains department," said Beryl.

"Can I come along when you study the catch?" Renny asked Beryl.

"Yes, yes, of course!"

CHAPTER XIII

Casting Off

EARLY the next morning before dawn, Mr. Thomas and Uncle Eddie were out with the other fishermen on the beach. They had just hauled in their big seine net and divided the sardines and other baitfish among themselves. Now they were loading last-minute fishing gear into their boats.

It was sunrise, and the sky was aflame with bright red and gold clouds. The water was calm, and waves lapped gently against the beach. There was a light breeze.

"Red sky at night, sailor's delight. Red sky at morn, sailors be warned," said Mr. Thomas quietly as he looked toward the east.

"Dey say de storm will stay to de nort," said Uncle Eddie.

"A-a. But still, I do not like de look of de sky," said Mr. Thomas.

"It look like de nor'easter might be gettin' too close-by," said one of the other fishermen.

"But de water *calm!* Dere's no *wind!*" said Buster Henry.

"De seas may be calm now, but they can change in a moment's time," answered Mr. Thomas. Rocky

Point was on the windward side of the island, where it was shallow and rough all the way to the reef wall, making it dangerous for boats, even in good weather. He didn't like it.

"So who makin' you de boss?" said Buster, putting his hands on his hips.

"A-a, man," said Gordy Smallbone, with a flick of his head. He was Buster's friend.

"Yeah, man, we tough. We boats is tough!" said Buster. The two of them started tossing spearguns and scuba tanks into their boats. "Alla-all-yuh can stay here. Gordy an' me go an' get alla dose tasty groupers!"

"A-a, man. Les' go fishin'!" chimed in Gordy.

And with that, they untied their lines from the sea grape trees, waded out, and hoisted themselves into their boats. They started their engines, and were off.

"Yeah, man. Let's go fishin'," rumbled others, as they also untied lines, pushed out their boats, climbed into them, and took off.

Mr. Thomas and Eddie Brown and a handful of fishermen stood there, watching the others leave. They rubbed their necks and looked at each other.

"Whatcha tink?" said Mr. Thomas.

They watched as the fishing boats disappeared from Cocoa Bay.

Finally, Eddie spoke. "I say we go ahead an' go. We can turn back if it starts to get too bad out dere. What if de storm does not come at all? Den we miss out on de best fishin' of de year."

CHAPTER XIV

The Problem With Groupers

R ENNY and Beryl walked along the beach at Cocoa Bay. It was late in the afternoon. The fishermen had all set forth for Rocky Point early that morning. Beryl wanted to see where the fishermen would be coming in, so she could plan for setting up her studies.

"Why do you measure them?" Renny asked Beryl.

"Well, we want to see how old they are. They don't mature and start spawning until they're over four years old—in fact, most of the time not even until they're six or seven. By then, they're pretty big fish. Since groupers get big enough to eat before they even mature, the fishermen keep them, not realizing the fish haven't yet reproduced.

"We also take special bones called otoliths out of their heads. We take them to the lab and do tests on them so we can accurately determine their ages. Sort of like counting tree rings to see how old a tree is. Then we can match the ages with their body lengths and weights. When we get enough data, we can start telling how old a fish is by its size and weight."

"So could a fisherman measure a fish and guess

his age?" said Renny.

"That's the idea. They pretty much keep growing as long as they're alive—although they do slow down considerably as they get older. But we could then tell fishers that they have to be at least a certain size before they can keep the fish. That way, we can be pretty sure a fish has been able to spawn at least a few times before it is taken."

"So it has a chance to have more young during its life," said Renny.

"Exactly. If you enjoy eating a certain kind of fish, you want there to be a good supply of it forever, right?"

"Yeah," said Renny.

Beryl continued, "Well, there's a big problem with the Nassaus: They're disappearing."

"They *are?*"

"They are. We're finding that most of the females caught still have eggs in their bellies—which means, of course, that the eggs haven't been shed before they've been caught. That's not good for future generations," said Beryl.

"My dad said the catch was way down last year. So the fishermen are going to try to catch more this year to make up for it," said Renny.

"Uh-oh," said Beryl. "That's another problem."

"Why?" said Renny.

Beryl took out a pen from her purse and began to draw on a piece of scrap paper.

"Okay. Let's back up a bit and suppose this: For many years, there are plenty of Nassaus. Tens of thousands in one aggregation! The only people fishing the aggregations are islanders feeding their own.

Even if the fish they catch still have eggs and milt in them, the fishing pressure is relatively light. So there really isn't much impact on the grouper population."

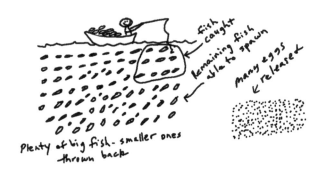

Plenty of big fish - smaller ones thrown back

"Are you with me?" said Beryl.

"Yeah," said Renny.

"Then the number of people on the island increases. Tourists come, eat the local food and go back home to tell everyone how good it tastes. Then they want to be able to eat it at home, so they ask for it in the grocery stores and the restaurants. Over the years, people all over the world are catching on to how good grouper tastes. So more and more grouper is demanded by the outside world," she continued.

"So now they have to start catching more grouper," said Renny.

"Exactly," said Beryl. "And as the demand for grouper goes up, so goes up the price of grouper. This is great news for the fish packing companies, who in turnwant to buy more fish from the fishers."

"And so the more fish the fishermen catch, the

more they can sell, and the more money they can make," added Renny.

"Yes. So the fishers catch more. After all, it's their livelihood. They're very happy to be able to supply more fish, especially if they can sell it all."

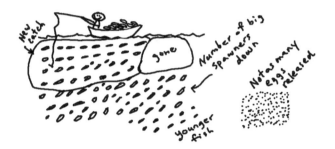

Beryl continued, "Okay. So remember, most of these fish are being taken before they've had a chance to spawn. Fishers keep taking out more spawners each year. When the number of spawners goes down, the number of eggs released each year goes down, too. What do you think is going to happen over time?"

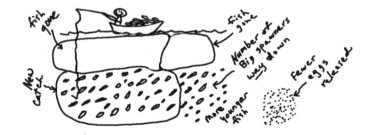

"If there aren't as many eggs, then there aren't as many new groupers being made to replace the ones that are caught," Renny said.

"Right. So then what happens to the population of Nassau groupers?" said Beryl.

"You mean the number of groupers," said Renny.

"Yes."

"That's easy. The number of groupers goes down," said Renny.

"Exactly," Beryl said. "Now add to that problem the fact that groupers take a long time to mature."

"You mean when they can reproduce?" asked Renny.

"Yes."

Renny thought for a minute. "Well, my dad says that the catch is down, and my mom says the Nassaus that are caught aren't as big as they used to be."

"You're on the right track. What do you think is happening?" said Beryl.

Renny thought some more. "The catch is going down because there aren't as many groupers."

"Yes—because most of the groupers that were caught in previous years couldn't first reproduce themselves, right?"

"Yeah," said Renny.

"OK, so we've established that fact. Now tell me why the Nassaus being caught aren't as big as they used to be."

Renny thought. Then he said, "The smaller fish are, the younger they are—and the bigger they are, the older they are, right?"

"Generally, yes."

"So if they're not as big as they used to be when they are caught, they're not as old, right?" said Renny.

"Yup."

"So does that mean there aren't as many of the bigger, older fish left?" asked Renny.

"It would seem so. And the bigger ones are the great spawners," said Beryl.

"So if the bigger, older ones are gone, all they're catching anymore are the younger ones, right?" said Renny.

"Yes, but remember what I said about groupers getting large before they mature?"

"Oh yeah. So even though they're big enough to be good eating, they're still young. And the younger ones are the only ones left. So the younger ones may never get the chance to to reproduce at all in their entire lives!" said Renny.

"Yes. And even if the younger ones do get a chance to spawn, they don't produce nearly as many eggs and as much milt as the older ones, who are gone. And because it takes so long for groupers to grow, the replacements are all getting caught before they can even replace themselves," said Beryl.

Renny's eyebrows shot up. "Pretty soon there won't be any more groupers at all!"

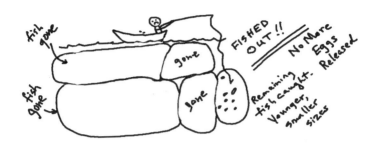

Beryl nodded. "Indeed, many of the Nassau grouper aggregations in other parts of the Caribbean have already been totally wiped out."

"Wow," said Renny. "Don't people understand what they're doing?"

"That's another problem. Some just don't think or care. They're only concerned for their short term benefits. Making money. But others just don't know. Overfishing can occur for years before anyone even realizes it—and when they do, it's often too late for the fish," said Beryl.

"What about the Nassaus on Macquerupa. Is it too late for them?" said Renny.

"We don't know. I hope not," replied Beryl.

"But don't fishermen understand what they're doing?" asked Renny.

"All the fishers know is that they can get top dollar for grouper. It's a chance to make a lot of money in a very short time. It's hard to pass up that kind of chance."

"But what good does it do to just wipe out all the groupers? Why can't they just take less fish?" asked Renny.

"Greed and ignorance. Some people are just very greedy. They don't know *when* to stop—or they don't want to stop. But even more important, many people just don't know. They don't understand that the life cycle of any grouper—or any other slow-growing fish for that matter, not just Nassaus—is extremely sensitive to overfishing."

"Why doesn't the government make them stop catching Nassau grouper?" said Renny.

"In U.S. waters, it is against the law to harvest Nassaus and jewfish at all. Jewfish are cousins to the Nassaus. They are proposing laws that apply to other grouper species in U.S. waters, too. But poaching is always a problem. That's when fishers catch them anyway, against the law. The law can be hard to enforce.

"But people still want grouper in their bellies. And because some Caribbean island nations still allow aggregation fishing, the fish companies just turn around and buy the fish from Caribbean countries. People who love eating grouper just don't want to give it up," Beryl said.

"Why don't the Caribbean governments outlaw Nassau grouper fishing, too?" Renny said.

"We're having a hard time making our own government understand that there's a problem. And they don't want to ruffle the feathers of the fishermen. Grouper Moon has been a very big fishing tradition for a very long time on Macquerupa—as on other islands. There would be a major revolt! Governments don't like revolts," said Beryl. "In the Cayman Islands, biologists are trying to get the government to close the grouper fishing season every other year. They think that might help the grouper stocks build up again, and still allow the fishing tradition to take place."

Renny was quiet.

Beryl continued, "Some island governments have made the spawning grounds off limits to using fish traps, which just suck in all kinds of reef fish. They're like vacuum cleaners on the reef. But then the fishermen just put their fish traps outside the spawning grounds. That way, they can catch groupers on their ways to the spawning grounds."

"But I thought governments were powerful! Why can't they just say, 'No more grouper fishing at all, and don't argue because we know best!' That's what my mom and dad always do to me," said Renny.

"And how does that make you feel when your parents tell you that?"

"Well, it does make me feel pretty stupid. As if they don't think that I can think for myself," admitted Renny. "Sometimes they probably do know better than me. But all they would have to do is tell me why they think so. And it might even make sense."

"So what you're saying is that if you are educated on a particular issue, you could make a responsible decision yourself, without somebody having to order you around," said Beryl.

"Yup," said Renny, standing up straighter.

Beryl looked out toward the sea. The breeze was picking up, and whitecaps were beginning to appear on the water. A look of concern crossed her face.

"I'm getting hungry. Why don't we start walking up to your mom's kitchen and get some dinner?" she said.

"It's too bad groupers taste so good," Renny said, as they walked toward the road.

"Yes. And as long as people want to eat them and are willing to pay for them, fish packers and fishers will find a way to supply them—until they are gone," said Beryl.

"So it's not only the fishermen's and the governments' faults, but also the people who want to eat them?" asked Renny.

"That's exactly right—in fact, even more so. If people stopped demanding so much grouper, the fish companies couldn't sell so much."

"So the fish companies wouldn't buy so much from the fishers," added Renny.

"Yes. And then the fishers wouldn't catch more than they could eat and sell. So the responsibility ultimately lies within each of us who eat the fish," said Beryl.

Renny became silent. He stared into the distance, lost in thought. Finally, he said, "But I thought each fish produced *tons* of eggs!"

"Oh, but they do! Some of the bigger fish can produce half a million eggs, or more. Of course, most of the bigger fish are gone, which leaves the smaller fish, who don't produce as many eggs."

"But there should still be plenty of young. It seems like we should be getting even *more* Nassaus," Renny countered.

"Ah. And therein lies another problem. Do you know what the spawn has to go through before they can even become young fish?" Beryl asked.

"Not exactly," said Renny.

"They have to endure incredibly hard times. Most of the eggs become food for other fish before they even have a chance to develop enough to settle in the turtle grass. If they make it that far, then the young ones have to keep from being eaten by bigger fish," said Beryl. She looked squarely at Renny. "Did you know that only one egg in several million actually survives to adulthood?"

Renny's eyebrows shot up. "Nah!!"

"Believe it or not," said Beryl.

Renny was silent. He thought about the Nassau grouper he had met at the drop-off. How lucky the fish was to have been able to survive as long as he did. He must be a very smart fish to have been able to outwit predators and humans, and become a top predator himself. Just think, he made it to the top— all the way out to the reef wall! Renny was filled with awe, and a new respect for his grouper.

CHAPTER XV

To Make a Difference

THE road began to climb and twist as it lead up the mountainside. The sky was starting to cloud over, and the breeze picked up from the northeast. Beryl and Renny walked and talked as they headed up to Renny's for dinner.

"I met a Nassau last week when I was skin diving," said Renny. "He was a nice fish."

"Oh, I'll bet it was beautiful!" said Beryl.

"Everyone else thinks Nassaus are ugly," said Renny, surprised. On that basis alone he decided that he might be able to trust Beryl. "Yeah, I thought he was real pretty. He was also very friendly." said Renny.

"Really?" said Beryl, looking at Renny.

"I almost speared him. I was just about to, but then he just disappeared. I'm glad, because I don't think I really could've speared him, anyway. He just sat there gazing at me straight in the eyes, all innocent and trustin'—as if the thought of getting speared never even crossed his mind," said Renny. "But then he sure fooled me. He just vanished right before my very eyes. And here I was supposed to bring home a Nassau for Christmas dinner."

"But I thought everyone ate pork for Christmas dinner around here," said Beryl.

"That's just what Mom said. But Dad said we would have seafood, too, 'cause J.D. was coming for dinner, and by golly J.D. just *loooves* Nassau grouper! J.D. gave me his old fins for Christmas. They are awesome. So I was supposed to spear a Nassau for dinner 'cause it is J.D.'s favorite. But now I'm extra glad I couldn't shoot the grouper. I would've killed him right before it was time for him to spawn," Renny said quietly, looking down.

"How big was it?" Beryl asked.

Renny held up his hands to indicate size. "About this big," he said.

"Hmmm. It's probably just around seven years old, then. This could be its first or second year of spawning," said Beryl.

"Wow. Then I might have killed him before he had been able to spawn at all in his life!" said Renny.

"He sounds like quite a fish," said Beryl.

"Yeah. His name is—" Renny caught himself. He still wasn't sure just how much he could trust Beryl, just yet.

Beryl looked at Renny quizzically.

Renny and Beryl continued walking as the road hairpinned up the mountainside. Ahead of them, a donkey chained to a stake on the roadside nibbled on the vegetation. It lifted up its head as the humans approached, and continued chewing.

"Hey big fella," said Renny patting the donkey's rump.

"Must be a boring life to have to be chained in

one place all day long," said Beryl. "But they do help keep back the jungle growth along the road."

"Yeah, but he's gonna be out of a job soon when the bulldozers get here," said Renny.

"Oh, and they are getting close!" said Beryl.

"I saw on the way to school before Christmas vacation where they had bulldozed, and mud was washin' into the sea. The water was turnin' orange," said Renny.

"Yes, and that's another problem for the fish. Not only are they overfished, but their habitat is in danger, too. The coral can recover when small amounts of silt from storms wash out. But when land is developed and the dirt isn't contained, way too much dirt washes into the sea, and it can smother the coral. And it also ruins the turtle grass beds, where all the babies are—remember?" said Beryl.

"Yeah." Renny sighed, and his shoulders dropped as he thought of J.D.'s planned resort at the top of Coconut Cove.

"They are planning two *huge* new resorts at the other end of the island. The land has been purchased by very rich developers," said Beryl. "They want to bring in thousands of tourists."

"All on this little island?" Renny stopped in his tracks.

"I'm afraid so," said Beryl. "Seems that everyone wants to flock to paradise."

"But too many people on our island will ruin it, and then no one will want to come anymore. Just the same way with reefs gettin' over-dived!" said Renny.

Beryl looked at Renny. "That's quite right. An island can take so much development, and support just so many people before everything starts to break down."

The sound of a horn honking from behind startled Beryl and Renny. A Jeep pulled alongside them.

"Hey y'all!" It was J.D..

"Hey," said Renny.

"Hi," said Beryl.

"Are y'all headed up to the house?"

"We're going up for dinner. Wanna come?" asked Renny.

Beryl looked at J.D. with interest. "Do I know you?" she asked.

Renny said, "Oh, this is J.D.—and this is Beryl. She's a fish biologist. She's here to study the grouper catch when it comes in."

"Pleased to meet you, ma'am," said J.D., grinning and tipping his hat.

"Likewise! So you're the one who loves to eat grouper," said Beryl. Her eyes brightened as she took J.D.'s hand.

"Yes, ma'am," he said. "There's nothin' better. I can't wait till they bring in the catch. Why don't you two hop in and I'll give you a ride up to the house."

They arrived at the house a few minutes later, where Margaret was getting ready for the evening's diners. Opal was helping.

Beryl, Renny, and J.D. sat down at a table on the porch. The sea breeze had picked up even more. It felt good.

"I love the view from here," said Beryl. The sky was clear as the sun began to set. The full moon was starting to rise in the east.

"Yeah, it's the greatest. I wonder if Renny and his folks know how lucky they are to have this spot. Right on the top of a mountainside, where they can see to the east, and to the north, and to the west. Best view on the island!" J.D. said.

"J.D. has the dive shop. He's going to build a dive resort at the top of Coconut Cove," said Renny.

"Really!" Beryl said. "The reefs here are some of the best in the Caribbean. You should do very well."

"I hope so. But I want to do it right. I don't want to wreck Renny's reef," said J.D., looking to Renny for approval.

But Renny's mind had started wandering to his latest reef encounter with the moray. He thought about the grouper and the green moray. Cooper and Maurice, of all names! Renny smiled to himself. He thought about what the Maurice had said, about Cooper venturing out to join the Nassau grouper aggregation, exposing himself, taking risks for the good of his own kind. He wondered if the grouper would return. Renny was worried.

J.D. didn't know what to make of Renny's silence. He decided not to press the boy, and turned to Beryl.

"So you're a fish biologist," he said.

"That's right," said Beryl. "I've been having quite an ongoing discussion with Renny over the last couple of days about grouper biology and fisheries. If we could educate everyone about the issues as I've been able to do with Renny, we might be able to get a handle on the problem."

"What problem?" asked J.D..

Renny's mind snapped to the present. "The Nassaus are gettin' all fished out. Pretty soon we're gonna have no more grouper if people like you don't stop likin' it so much," Renny blurted.

J.D. reeled. "Well, blow me down! Do I detect just a wee bit of hostility in those words?"

Renny looked down. "Sorry," he said.

"Well, I honestly don't know if I could live my life another minute knowing I couldn't eat another Nassau grouper. But why don't you tell me exactly what it is about my enjoyment of a nice, big, fat juicy grouper that is ruining the world," said J.D..

Beryl casually covered her mouth with her hand as she tried to suppress a smile. She looked at Renny and nodded. "Why don't you fill this good man in on the news?"

Renny's mother had appeared, wondering what was going on. Opal came, too. They sat down.

Renny proceeded to relate what he had learned about the groupers. The small group listened with respect, surprised at the passion with which the boy spoke.

"Oh, my," said Opal when Renny was finished, "I had no idea!" She was thinking about who she would tell first.

"So that's why I can't get as many servings out of a Nassau anymore," said Margaret. She thought of her sign by the road, advertising the soon-to-come grouper, and sighed.

J.D. was thoughtful. "Well, I can see that I am gonna have to re-educate my taste buds. It's gonna be awfully hard." He sighed, too.

It was now dark. The breeze had become a light wind. Margaret glanced toward the east with concern. Clouds had started to obscure the full moon.

Beryl said, "Well, most of us are guilty of not worrying about our resources until they're almost gone. Perhaps peoples' love of grouper will help save the fish. The Senegalese ecologist, Baba Dioum, once said, *"In the end we will conserve only what we love; we will love only what we understand; and we will understand only what we are taught."*

The group was quiet.

"So if we are to help everyone in the world to understand, all of us are going to have to come out of our safe little caves, even if it means sticking out our necks," said Renny.

The adults all turned to Renny in surprise.

"*That* is the opinion of a very wise person," said Beryl.

"And where did you come up with somethin' like that?" said Opal.

Renny grinned. "In a cave."

He thought about how Maurice had helped him understand what he needed to do. Renny didn't think he needed to share the details with the grown-ups. But he had started thinking about how he might be able to help make a difference for the groupers.

"Well, like it or not, Macquerupa has been noticed by the world," J.D. said. "Dive bookings are coming in. How can we use this to our advantage? What would you say about starting to educate every tourist who comes to the island? Then encourage them to go back and spread the word?"

"That would certainly be a start," Beryl said. "Educating our own people will be enough of a challenge in itself. It's not easy to change something that's been a way of life for many years."

"Yeah. And my craving for grouper isn't gonna disappear overnight, either." J.D. sighed.

"When I'm a dive guide for J.D., I'm gonna make sure everyone I take on the reef is very careful," Renny said. "And I'm gonna tell them all about the groupers."

"So does that mean you'll work for me?" J.D. turned toward Renny.

"Yeah. I'll be a dive guide for you," said Renny. "I'll share my reef with others, teach them to take care of it, and make them love it, too. Then they'll want to keep it safe."

"And then they'll want to keep all the reefs of the world safe," added Beryl. "You *will* be making a difference, Renny. It all starts with individuals."

"Like buildin' a reef, polyp by polyp—only I hope savin' groupers doesn't take as long," said Renny.

A sudden gust of wind whipped the tablecloth and scattered napkins around the porch.

Everyone looked eastward. "That nor'easter isn't supposed to come nearly this close," said J.D.. "I wonder what's going on?"

CHAPTER XVI

The Big Bash

"Yo, Coop!"

"Huh?" grunted the sleepy grouper.

"Wake up and get your tail over here!" It was Louie. Another morning was breaking. Louie motioned Cooper over with the wave of a pectoral fin. He and several of his cohorts were huddled together.

"Guys, this is Coop. He's new to the group," said Louie.

"Hey," said Cooper, to the small group.

"Yo." "Heya." "Howerya doin'?" "Nice tie." "Whaddaya need ta know?" they said in turn.

"It's all so new, and incredible, too. What a gathering this is. And whoa—take a look at that view!" Cooper said, as he swung around to survey the area.

Daylight filled the reef below the promontory. Even more Nassau groupers had joined the gathering. Cooper never even dreamed that so many of his kind existed. Most were milling about, catching up on old times. Some were already in small groups playing chase, or circling each other, chasing tails.

Cooper watched intently. The chasers had on new outfits: a black topcoat with a white belly. He thought it looked quite nice.

"It's the party tux. Watch closely—for awhile, they will change in and out of their party colors." said Uncle Epinephelus. He had seen Cooper watching the activity and come up to join him. They were both still in their stripes.

"It's hard to tell, as they circle and bend, who's after whom—who's chasing whose end," said Cooper, as he watched.

"And so it is. But it's just the start. You've seen *nothing!* It'll tickle your heart, when all of us dance as the sun sets just right—it's a most glorious time— and a splendid sight!" said the old fish. Then he added, with a worried look to the water's surface, "That is, if we even get to dance..."

"Why do you say that?" Cooper wanted to know. He turned toward Epinephelus.

"There should be many times more of us here by now," the huge grouper said, "And the sky doesn't look right. If we can't see the sun, we can't dance tonight."

"What do you mean, there should be more of us here? I've never seen so many Nassaus before in my whole entire life! I didn't even *know* there were so many of us," Cooper replied.

"Oh, this is nothing compared to what it used to be like," Uncle Epinephelus said. "There used to be hundreds more of us!"

"Really?! Why aren't there so many of us now?"

"We're all getting caught by the humans."

"Why would the humans want *us?*"

"Because we taste good. Too good. We just taste too good. They can't get enough of us. We're a delicacy—a choice food."

"You mean, just as crabs are a favorite food for me?" Cooper asked. He hadn't even thought of crabs for the last couple of days. The thought of crabs awakened his hunger.

"Yup. And as a nice bluestriped grunt is to me. We all like what we like. And humans like *us.*"

Cooper pondered this. He had never been faced with a human who had wanted to eat him before. He thought about Buck. But he had sensed no real threat from this boy. Weren't all humans the same?

Uncle Epinephelus continued, "We're harder for humans to catch because we're loners. But every now and then one of us'll get nailed with a spear. I've had some near-misses myself. It seems that the bigger I've gotten, the more I've had to watch my tail."

"Whoa. But I just like *little* crabs. The big ones make my belly hurt," said Cooper.

"They like us big—the bigger, the better. But they've already caught most of us big ones, so now they'll take us however they can get us. By nature we're friendly and trusting—and curious, too. And that's part of our problem."

"Why?"

"Because many humans, the ones with tanks—especially the ones without spears—think we're pretty cute. They just want to be friends and feed us and pet us. So we get used to them being friendly and all, and we start to enjoy hanging with them. But then along comes one with a spear. That just takes all the fun out of it." Epinephelus turned toward Cooper. "Beware of the one who has a speargun. You must learn to beware of the human with a speargun. We already know to watch out for cudas and sharks. But the humans can fool us. We have to watch our tails."

Cooper pondered this for a bit. So that was a speargun Buck pointed at me that time? Hmmm. But I still don't think he would've shot me. Then Cooper said, "But if we're solitary sorts and hard to catch, there can't be too many of us missing from being speared, right?"

"True. Except we start to trust them, and then we get fooled. But I suppose if a few of us are lost to the occasional spear, well, it's really not that big a deal in the grand scheme of things. Unless you're the one getting speared, of course. Then it's a pretty big deal. But that's life. We're born, we live, we hope to reproduce, we die. All living creatures have to eat to live. *We* have to eat, too..."

"But there are *lots* of little crabs!" Cooper cried.

"Yes, and there used to be a lot of us Nassaus. But now there are not many of us. During recent times humans have caught on to our annual party. They used to not bother us so much. But now, they're all over the place! Just look around and see all those hooks and lines. And even divers with tanks and spears. We're easy to catch here, because we're not watching our own tails. We get caught while watching others' tails. And then they bait us with the tastiest of delicacies: live sardines."

Cooper moved out from beneath the ledge and looked up. Sure enough, hooks with tantalizing sardines were hanging in the water.

"Mmmm! I have a feeling. I have a hunch, that my belly would *love* such a morsel for lunch!" said Cooper. He thoughtlessly headed up to grab one.

"And if you take that morsel, I have a strong hunch that some human belly will have *you* for lunch!" the wise old fish snapped as he lunged out to stop the hungry grouper.

Cooper returned to the shelter of the ledge. He felt foolish.

"Not only do you have to watch your tail, but you must keep your head, too," instructed Uncle Epinephelus.

"It's not fair," sighed Cooper. "Why do they want so many of us?"

"I don't know. Maybe they're all gluttons for grouper. Maybe there are too many of them."

Cooper thought of the boy. He didn't seem like a glutton. But then again, he did have more lobsters in his bag than it seemed he could have eaten in one meal.

"Come with me. But be careful! Watch your tail—and keep your head," warned Uncle Epinephelus.

The big, older fish led the smaller, younger fish back up the reef wall to the promontory, away from the party. There came into sight something that the younger fish had never seen before.

Cages. Everywhere. Cages filled with Nassau grouper. There were bones of smaller fishes at the bottoms of the cages. The groupers all had their noses pressed to the wire mesh of the cages.

Cooper became sad and afraid. "Whoa. Can't we help them get out?"

"There's nothing we can do to help. Once they go in they're goners."

"You mean they just go into those things? Why would they do a thing like that?"

"Curiosity. We're curious fish, remember? And to eat. The humans bait them with smaller fish. The bigger fish enter, thinking they're going to get an easy meal. Then that's it. They're trapped. And all they can do is stare outside and think about how they were conned."

Cooper felt helpless. He wished he could help the trapped fish escape.

"You think this is bad? This is nothing. You wanna *really* see something? Come with me."

Uncle Epinephelus led Cooper to shallower water. There they found the biggest cage of all. It was filled with hundreds of Nassau groupers. Most of them had their snouts pressed against the wire mesh as well, looking unhappy about having been caught.

Above the surface, humans could be seen tossing more groupers into the huge cage from their boats. Most of the fish were alive—some bleeding from where they had been hooked or speared, but many who had been trapped were unhurt. A few continued to chase each other around in circles.

"This is where they keep us until they're done fishing," said the old fish.

The two free groupers swam around the holding pen, surveying the situation. Cooper was hoping to find a rip in the mesh that might provide a means of escape. The cage was so big, and there were no holes. It seemed hopeless.

The surge started to pick up. The fish in the holding pen rocked with the surge. Those who had noses to the mesh were starting to get bumped. Cooper and Epinephelus started to swim away from the swaying cage. Just then, Cooper heard a familiar voice.

"Coopie?"

Cooper turned back toward the voice. His eyes rapidly rotated. His heart jumped into his gullet. His stomach turned flip-flops and his belly went white.

"Sadie?"

There she was, on the other side of the wire mesh.

Cooper's heart sank at the sight of Sadie, trapped in the holding pen.

"Coopie? Oh, I knew it was you by the wag of your tail. You have the cutest little wag! Oh, I'm *so* glad you are here." But then she was distracted. Looking hard at Cooper's chin, she said, "Coopie, what is with that crab hanging from your neck?"

"Huh?" said Cooper.

Henry the neck crab decided that things were now just too close for his comfort. Oh, boy, he thought, and this was all for *her.* What nerve. And *he* never figured out I was even here. What a fish. "My dear esteemed grouper," announced the neck crab, "it is time for me to *vamoose! I* am *outa* here. Hasta la *veeesta!"*

"Never mind, it's gone now," said Sadie. "Coopie, can't you do something to help us get out of this contraption?

Cooper turned to Uncle Epinephelus, who shook his head.

Cooper was despondent. He could not understand why he had to come all this way to find Sadie, especially when she lived right in the next territory. And here she was. Caught. It all seemed so pointless. Cooper didn't know what to do.

"How did you get caught?" Cooper said.

"I did the stupidest thing. I was so hungry, and about to ambush a tasty little fish when it swam into one of those cages. And there I went, right after it without even thinking. What a dummy I was!"

"Don't you worry, I'll stay right here with you,

Sadie. We'll think of something. There's gotta be something we can do!" said Cooper, with resolve.

Uncle Epinephelus shook his head slowly. "I don't think so," he said, quietly.

The old fish was sad. He was recalling what it used to be like, when the reef was full of Nassaus. There had been so many Nassaus at the big annual dance that he couldn't even see them all. It was awesome. Life was good then. There were lots of big old, wise groupers like himself. They would swap stories about their years and their lives. Now Epinephelus had few peers left. He was the biggest, oldest grouper at this year's party. He missed his old cronies. He was tired and depressed.

"I'm just an old fish, Coop. Just an old fish. I used to be so excited about coming to the big bash. Now things are just not the way they're supposed to be. They're not the same. We're all getting caught.

"And now the sky is too dark. If there are any of us still left, we won't even get a chance to dance if we can't see when the sky looks right. If we can't dance, we can't spawn—and if we can't reproduce..." the old fish's voice trailed off. Then he said, "The future just doesn't bode well for us Nassaus."

"Why do we have to come all this way to have our young? Why couldn't Sadie and I just pair up on our own reef and have a normal family life?" Cooper asked.

Epinephelus replied, "Well, what's normal for fishes?" He thought a bit. Then he continued, "Lots of different things are normal. What *is* a normal family life? A mom and dad and a bunch of their little fish fry swimming around them? Maybe for a damselfish.

"A dad brooding a clutch of eggs in his mouth until they hatch, while their mother is God-knows-where? Maybe for a jawfish.

"Guys and gals just meeting every night at sunset to dance, and casting their spawn to the currents? Maybe for hamlets.

"Ladies and gentlefish meeting once a year and casting *their* spawn to the currents? That's us. Normal for us is living alone on the reef, each in one's own territory. We're top dogs on the reef. The life of a top dog is a solitary existence.

"But we have to reproduce, just like every other living thing. So this is what we do. We all get together once a year to spawn, in a place where our young can have the best chance of getting off to a good start. Nature has made it that way, and Nature doesn't have to explain herself. Why we all gather at this precise place and time, I haven't a clue. But we do. And that's the way it is," said Uncle Epinephelus.

"What happens to our young?" asked Cooper.

"Who knows? I've never come across any of what I recognize to be our small fry. But every now and then I run into some of our youngsters on the patch reefs. I don't remember my life before the patch reefs. Do you? You're a lot closer to that time of life than I am," said Epinephelus.

"I don't think I have have even given it any thought until now," said Cooper.

Suddenly, there was a big surge. The fins of both fish all sprang out in alarm as they were swept against the wire mesh of the big cage.

"Ouch!" a startled Cooper yelled.

"Uh-oh, it's getting too rough. This is *not* good," said Uncle Epinephelus.

The surge continually grew stronger. The fish inside the holding pen were being swept back and forth into the wire mesh sides. Cooper and Uncle Epinephelus swam away from the cage again and kept their distance. They could hear grunts and groans coming from the fish trapped inside the holding pen. The wire mesh began to move up and down with the surge. The surface of the water sizzled with pouring rain. The sky was almost black.

The force of the surge continued to grow. Swells began to break on the reef, making the water at the surface white and foamy.

"We should head for deeper water," Uncle Epinephelus warned.

"Don't leave us, Coopie!"

Cooper was determined to stay with Sadie. "You can go back—but I'm staying here!"

"Well then, my friend, if you're staying, then so am I. But we should at least get under a coral head. We'll be of no use to the others if we're hurt," Uncle Epinephelus said. They took shelter under a small patch of coral. Space was tight, but they were protected from the violent surge. From there they could still see the holding pen as it swayed to and fro. Then they heard the sounds of boat engines passing overhead, and fading in the distance.

"Are the humans leaving?" Cooper asked.

"It must be getting too rough for them up there." Epinephelus said, with hope.

The big pen creaked and groaned as it rocked back and forth in the rough surge. The fish inside grew more and more agitated. A section of mesh brushed against a huge stand of elkhorn coral and became entangled. The coral held fast to the mesh as the rest of the big pen of fish whipped around. Cooper heard the cage scrape against the coral. Large chunks of coral that were caught in it started to break off. Suddenly, Cooper's fins jumped out.

"Hey! Look at the cage!" he exclaimed, "The cage is starting to rip!...Oh my!...oh *my* ... whoa, boy! It's getting bigger ... oh, it's gonna be a *big* rip!"

The rip grew as the cage was pulled and torn by the sharp, hard coral in the violent surge. Cooper swam out from his sheltered spot toward the holding pen, swishing back and forth, trying to navigate the rough water.

"Sadie! ...look! You can get out! Hey, Nassaus! Look! ...over here! You can get out!" he called to the distressed groupers.

Sadie and several of the trapped fish found their way to the rip in the cage. It was hard to get near enough to it without smashing into the coral.

"Stay back and watch for when the torn part is swept away from the coral!" Uncle Epinephelus called in his deep voice.

One by one, the groupers made their way out against the surge. Then there was a final BANG as the cage broke free of the reef, taking big chunks of coral with it. It was easier to get out after that, and soon there was a crowd of Nassau groupers waiting to file out of the holding pen. Out they streamed, one by one—then by pairs. Many were dazed and confused, and some were bleeding from their wounds. But soon they were all free.

"Hey, maybe the other cages are getting torn up, too—let's go see!" said Cooper.

Sure enough, the traps had also been tumbling about in the strong surge, and had started to break apart, freeing more fish. They all headed for deeper water.

"Oh, this is delicious!" Epinephelus muttered. Then he bellowed, "Come on *every*one! Come on out if you can! Squeeze through the rips! Squeeze through the tears! Come on *down!* There's gonna be a ball!"

But in all the confusion, they didn't notice a new danger. Attracted by the blood and the commotion of the great grouper escape, a natural predator had appeared on the scene. Wounded, bleeding groupers were snapped up before they could know what had hit them.

"Sharks! Hey! *Watch out for sharks!*"

With booms, the groupers all scattered, heading for whatever cover they could find. Some headed for the reef bottom and snugged themselves against or under coral heads. Some headed for the safety of ledges and crannies in the nearby reef wall. They turned back and watched, aghast, as wounded fish, who couldn't move fast enough, were picked off by the sharks.

"Oh my," mourned Uncle Epinephelus. "This *isn't*

good. I abhor the smell of blood."

Cooper, Sadie and Epinephelus watched in horrified silence, as the forces of Nature took care of its injured and dying.

"At least those who died by the shark were able to die instantly and with dignity," Cooper said, sadly. He hoped it would be that way for him when his time came. He hoped all the crabs and little fish that *he* took didn't have to suffer.

Uncle Epinephelus cast a worried look to the surface. "If the sky stays dark, we won't know when the time is right to dance. This isn't good. All this for nothing. Our struggles will have been in vain if we can't even dance. *Oh, what aggravation to this aggregation!"* he howled.

With their bellies full, the sharks started to dissipate, but the frightened groupers remained in their shelters.

"I wonder what time of day it is, anyway," Sadie said. With her belly full of eggs, she was uncomfortable and anxious to shed them. Others, also fidgety with swelling bodies, were eager for the dance to begin. But they couldn't dance until it was time— when the currents would carry the spawn out to sea at twilight—when it would be hard for predators to see the eggs. Everything had to be just so. That was one of the challenges of being a fish specie who spawns only once a year.

"Sadie, do you think any of our young will come back to our reef? Do you think they will recognize us?" Cooper asked.

Sadie replied, "They may recognize us as being one of their own kind, but they won't be our own young. They will be the children of us all. When we dance, we all release our spawn. My eggs may be fertilized by milt from other Nassaus. That's the way Nature made it happen. It's better for our kind that way."

"Whoa," said Cooper. He wondered if he would ever understand Nature's way. He wondered why he should even care, if that's the way it was supposed to be for the Nassaus.

But then, he was a curious fish, and he did care. Perhaps he had too much time to lay around watching other fish on his reef. He wondered if he should be doing anything more productive with his life. Maybe he shouldn't use the morning changeover to think so much. Maybe that was his problem. Maybe he should just lighten up, as Sam the parrotfish had told him to do. Wouldn't his life be a lot simpler for him if he didn't care?

"But that's what I like about you, Coopie, besides your cute wag. You *do* care," said Sadie. "If I were a motherly fish, I would want you to be there for our young."

Cooper blushed and squirmed. "Well, maybe being top dog in my territory keeps me busy enough. Maybe it's good that I don't have my own young. I wouldn't want to spread my responsibilities too thinly," Cooper said. "But it sure seems like it would be nice." He sighed, thinking of the sargeant majors.

They became quiet. Most of the rest of the group were quiet, too. Some of the restless ones began to play chase, but their efforts were half-hearted. Uncle Epinephelus just sat on his tail, depressed and deep in thought.

But suddenly, the silence was broken. "Say, *look!*" they heard a grouper exclaim. "It's getting brighter!"

"Hey, the sky is getting light again!" yelled the group of groupers under the next coral head. They yelled to the next group, who in turn yelled to the *next* group. Soon there was again a spirited optimism among the Nassau grouper aggregation.

Uncle Epinephalus came to life again. This is *good!* he thought. He looked toward the surface. It wouldn't be very long now.

And finally, when the sun began to disappear and the light in the water was just so, he announced what everyone had been waiting to hear.

"Say, it's time to get ready to dance! I do believe it's time! Papa *Yo!* Hey everyone, let's *boogie!*"

CHAPTER XVII

The Dance

IT was almost sunset. The big group headed for deeper water. Some of the males changed into their black and white tuxedos and began to chase females who had changed into solid dark outfits. More Nassaus in their party colors joined in. When the group was deep enough, some of the dance leaders started to spiral up toward the surface in the water. Soon there was a big whorl of circling fish, growing ever wider as more fish joined the dance.

It was sunset. From the bottom, Cooper and Sadie watched in awe as the whirling mass took on the appearance of a gigantic column, wide at the bottom, and narrowing toward the top. Small groups of spiraling fish spun off and then came together at the top to release their gametes into the water. Around and around and up it grew—a big, wide vortex of black and white.

Cooper was entranced. Uncle Epinephelus was thoughtful. It was an extraordinary sight.

"Come on, Coopie! Let's dance!" exclaimed Sadie, nudging Cooper. Cooper changed into his tux, and Sadie her black gown, as Cooper started to chase Sadie. They circled around each other several times before entering the dance at the bottom of the circling mass.

Time to Boogie

"Hey group, it's Coop!"

There were Louie and his cohorts, in their tuxedos. They joined Cooper as they spiraled upward, chasing after Sadie. They all came together and released their spawn into the water at the top of the spiraling mass, before scattering and diving back down to the bottom. Cooper was euphoric. So this is what it was all about! This is what Nature had intended.

"Let's dance again, Sadie! Come, Uncle Epinephelus, join us!" Cooper shouted excitedly.

As Uncle Epinephelus entered the dance, the others parted out of respect for their oldest and wisest. The big grouper spiraled lazily upward, savoring the swim. He and Cooper were joined at the top by Sadie and other females, before they all separated and swam back down to the bottom.

The dance began to wind down soon after sunset.

"Whoa. I'm bushed!" Cooper finally admitted.

All of the groupers were exhausted. It had been a long, tiring and frightening day. But it had ended well for most of them. They had been able to spawn. Nature had made the skies dark and the seas rough to scare away the fishers. Nature had made the seas rough enough to rattle and tear up the cages so that the trapped fish could escape. Nature had then parted the clouds, to allow the fish to see the sky and know when the time was right to dance.

"Isn't Nature splendid!" Cooper thought. Even if he didn't understand it. Would they be this lucky next time around? Would the humans be back with their cages, and hooks and sardines, and spears? Would they be able to escape again?

Cooper hoped there would be a next time for him. Knowing the game of life and death on the reef, he knew that at any time he could become food for a shark or barracuda—or a human—just as crabs were food for him. But he loved life, and hoped he would be able to survive long enough to become a wise old fish like Uncle Epinephelus.

"We're done," said Uncle Epinephelus the next morning, at daybreak. "Our mission has been accomplished. Now it is time to return to our own homes."

Most of the groupers started leaving in groups. Sadie, Louie and his cohorts, Cooper, Uncle Epinephelus and others started back toward shallower water to catch the drop-off. There were ripped up cages strewn around, and broken-off chunks of coral everywhere. Fishing line entangled the coral. The reef was littered with trash from the humans. They passed a plastic bag filled with feces.

"Yuck." "What a mess." "Gross and disgusting!" The fish surveyed the scene.

"I don't think I even *want* to come back to this place again," said Louie.

"Yeah. Nature saved our tails this time around. But is this what we get to look forward to next time? Ugh."

They turned to Uncle Epinephelus, who was lost in thought, for an answer. He always had answers.

But this time, he did not.

CHAPTER XVIII

Waiting

RENNY, J.D., Beryl, Margaret, and Opal all sat on the porch drinking coffee and cocoa tea, their eyes cast eastward. The storm had been bad. It had cleared briefly around sunset, and then struck again with a vengeance during the night. Now it was midday. The sky had cleared, and they were awaiting word from the fishermen.

"It is rough on Rocky Point, but close enough to the main island. They should have been able to get back to land quickly enough before it got bad," said Beryl.

"But it is rocky and the reef is shallow there. And if they made it to shore, their boats may have been wrecked on the beach. It is not a protected beach," said Aunt Opal.

"And it is just like you to imagine the very worst," snapped her sister, Margaret. "Why do you have to be like that?"

J.D. spoke. "I'm sure they would have seen the storm coming. Your husbands are sensible men. They would have had the sense to leave the fishing grounds in time," he said. "So let's all assume they are safe. If their boats were wrecked on the beach, then they'll find another way to get back home."

"I wonder about Buster Henry and his friends. They don't have any sense," said Renny.

Beryl was quiet. She was concerned for the fishermen. But she was also worried about the groupers. If they were in traps and holding pens during the storm, they would be thrashed against the sides, and might be harmed. Would they become shark food? She shuddered at the thought.

On the other hand, perhaps by some miracle the groupers had been able to get free. Would they still have been able to spawn? It would be difficult to know. She began to secretly hope so.

"Beryl?" Renny asked quietly.

"Yeah," answered Beryl.

"What are you thinking?" Renny said.

"I'm thinking that everything is going to be just fine." She smiled at Renny.

A light blue pickup truck pulled into the driveway. Out of the cab jumped a government official with navy blue shorts and a white shirt. Everyone on the porch stood up. Margaret felt faint and grabbed her sister's arm to steady herself. J.D. put his arm around Margaret.

"Hello!" said the official. It was Wilfred Kingsley, from the police department. He was an old friend.

"Hello. Any word on what's happening?" J.D. asked.

"I just wanted to come by to let you know that your husbands are fine. Their boat took on some damage, but they think it's fixable. They're working on it now, and helping some of the others with repairs. They'll head on back when they're done. We took them some supplies. It might be tomorrow before they return, though. But I just wanted to let you know that they're okay."

Margaret and Opal sat back down, and let out huge sighs of relief. "Thank goodness," they both said.

"See what I told you?" J.D. smiled. Then he turned back to Wilfred. "What about the others?"

"There were quite a number of them out there, even from other islands, it seems. Apparently most of them came into shore before it got too bad, but there were some stubborn ones, and a few may be missing. We won't know for sure for awhile," said Wilfred.

"What about Buster?" said Renny.

"Buster's okay. A couple of his friends got hurt pretty badly, though. We took them to the hospital. But they'll be okay."

Beryl sighed. "Good. What about the fish?"

"Well, they were able to take a couple of boats back out to check the holding pens this morning. The pens were beat up pretty badly, and the fish were gone. They couldn't check the traps, though. But they're sending some divers down to check. I never saw such a bunch of unhappy fishermen in my life." said Wilfred, shaking his head. "Well, I'd better go let the other families know. See you later."

"Thanks for coming, Wilfred," said Margaret.

They all returned to their coffee and cocoa tea, and talked about the events of the last couple of days.

"Beryl?" said Renny.

"Yeah."

"What do you think about the fish?" said Renny.

"Well, I'm hopeful. But I don't think we'll ever know for sure. If anything, maybe it'll buy them a little time," said Beryl.

"Maybe we can help the groupers. Like come up with some big plan or something like that to save them," said J.D..

"Well, we know that will be easier said than done," said Beryl. "It's going to take time, and we have our work cut out for us. But we have to start somewhere."

"Well, I know where I'm going to start," said Margaret. She got up from her chair and walked across the porch. Then she disappeared down the driveway. She returned a few minutes later with her sign and leaned it against the railing.

"There'll be no more grouper served from this kitchen for a long time. Too bad. It was the best on the island. I'll have to come up with something else that tastes good," Margaret said.

"Oh, you will, dear. You always do," said her sister, patting her hand. "And I am going to go right down to the library to schedule a village council meeting. And Beryl, dear, you will be the speaker. We are going to do some rabble-rousing."

"Gladly!" grinned Beryl.

"Well, tourists are coming in just a couple of weeks. What do you think, Renny? Should we get started on those scuba lessons?" J.D. said.

"Yeah, man!" said Renny, giving J.D. a high-five.

"J.D., what are your plans for your dive resort?" asked Beryl.

"Well, for starters, I have enough maney to build a small hotel, and I want to do a few improvements on the property to spruce it up a bit," said J.D..

"Well, I hope you will remember that preserving habitat for our fish and wildlife is critical. And you will be careful to take appropriate measures before you do any digging to keep the dirt contained, won't you? We can't have it running off to smother our reefs," Beryl said.

"Oh, for sure! I want to do it right," J.D. said.

"And you won't take sand from the beach to make concrete?" said Beryl.

"Oh no, ma'am, I won't," said J.D..

"You'll educate yourself on all island environmental issues, and work with us to keep our island from getting ruined, won't you?" said Beryl.

"Oh yes, ma'am, I will!"

"And I'll be meeting with government officials to see about what we can do to control island development before it is too late. We need to come up with a good plan that will be good for us economically, but will at the same time sustain our island resources. We don't want to overdevelop our island," said Beryl.

"I'll do what I can to help," said J.D..

"Have you ever thought about hosting marine science camps for kids or anything like that? Educating the public is a good thing, but if we're going to try to change attitudes, we can't forget the kids. They can be quite persuasive," said Beryl, smiling at Renny. Renny grinned back.

"Good idea," said J.D.. "But we'll need to keep the costs down, so people can afford to come here with their kids. Maybe we could even set up some kind foundation or something for public education and outreach."

"There you are talking big money," said Beryl. "*That* will be hard to come by."

"Well, who knows? When I was a kid here, it was rumoured that pirates hid an old barrel full of Spanish bullion out there somewhere. A barrel, of all things! Maybe we'll get lucky and find it," said J.D.. He caught Renny's eye and winked.

Renny's eyebrows shot *way* up.

CHAPTER XIX

A Good
Place to Be

A FEW mornings later when the weather and sea had settled, Renny slipped away to the cove. He sat alone on the beach. Studying the old concrete dressing room foundation, he wondered how anything could be rebuilt on it. He looked toward the old pilings and tried to imagine a platform full of scuba gear.

Renny donned his mask, fins and snorkle. He plunged into the water and headed for the drop-off. Finding the markers he'd left before, he followed the sand channel and sand chute to the grotto. Taking a deep breath, he dived to the opening, and carefully slid through it. He relaxed. He loved this place.

"You're back." Maurice the moray brushed against Renny.

"Hey there, big fella." Renny stroked the eel.

"Say, follow me!" The eel slithered against Renny and led the way through the school of silversides, to the grotto opening on the reef wall.

There, sitting on the old barrel, was a familiar Nassau grouper, sitting on his tail and enjoying the view before him.

"Heya, Coop! You made it back! I'm so glad."

"Hey yourself, Buck."

Renny lay down on his belly and started to gently clear the sand away from the barrel. He found a hole near the top of it, on the side facing the wall of the grotto. He tried to peer inside, but it was too dark. Carefully, he stuck his hand through the hole. It barely fit. Reaching in as far as his arm was allowed, Renny felt around. All he could feel was sand. Suddenly, something clamped down hard on his finger.

"What th—!" yelped Renny. He yanked his hand out of the hole, ripping his finger from the clutches of whatever had taken hold of it. Renny instinctively stuck his finger in his mouth.

Then his eye caught something scratched in the side of the barrel. With his free hand, Renny cleared more sand away so he could read it. It said, "John David Patrick was here."

Renny grinned. He knew then that J.D. understood—and could be trusted.

At the top of the cove, J.D. stood near the pile of concrete rubble with his hands in his pockets. He had watched Renny as he snorkeled out to the reef and disappeared in the water. J.D. wasn't worried about the boy. Lost in thought, he was recalling his own boyhood days on the same reef, when he had discovered a secret grotto where he didn't have to breathe, and he could communicate with fish. But now he was too big to fit through the entrance.

"Savor your time there, Renny, because soon you'll be grown. And don't worry, I'll take good care of our reef. Your secret will be safe with me."

J.D. smiled.

A few months later...

Cooper sat on his barrel, taking in the changeover, surveying his territory. Everything was in order. All denizens were accounted for, and the grouper's bones felt fine. He was thinking about the fun he and Maurice had had the night before, hunting together. They had a game, where Cooper would lay in the sand at the base of a coral head. Then Maurice would enter the coral head from the other side, flushing the choicest of little crabs out the opening where Cooper waited to ambush them. It was now Cooper's favorite time of the day. He loved hunting the coral heads with Maurice.

The changeover was finished, and the day shift on the reef was in full swing. Cooper decided to take a stroll through his territory. He swam back through the grotto, and headed up the sand channel.

His eye caught sight of a familiar fish lounging under a coral head, and he headed toward her.

"Hey, Sadie," said Cooper. His color intensified.

"Hi, Coopie!" Sadie turned dark on the top, and her belly turned white. She tilted to the side.

They flashed their teeth at each other. Then they went their separate ways.

Later on, as Cooper was waiting in line to be cleaned at his favorite cleaning station, he heard a familiar voice.

"Hey, Coopie! Come with me." It was Sadie again. She motioned with her pectoral fin and swung her head and tail. "Come, quickly!"

Cooper followed her through the patch reefs, almost to the turtle grass beds. There was an area of coral rubble and sand. She stopped at a solitary clump of branched coral that was nearly overgrown and surrounded by delicate buff-colored algae. There, dancing in and out of the coral fingers, was a small group of tiny juvenile Nassau groupers. They retreated into the coral fingers as Sadie and Cooper approached.

Cooper and Sadie looked at each other and smiled. Then Sadie left.

But Cooper stayed, and waited patiently until the little groupers cautiously reappeared, one by one. Keeping their wary eyes on Cooper, they hovered just near the tips of the coral fingers.

"Hello, little groupies!" Cooper said softly.

He settled back on his tail. He couldn't take his eyes off the tiny Nassau groupers.

"It fills me inside, from my tail to my nose. This feeling of gladness, inside me it grows. How I do love my life on this reef in the sea! Welcome, my friends—it's a good place to be."

The End

On a personal note...

My husband, Tim, and I have been scuba diving since the early nineteen-seventies. Both being underwater photographers, our noses are always in our own respective subject matter when we're diving. I remember dives in the earlier years where I'd glance over to see what Tim was shooting, and think, "Oh, it's just another Nassau." Anymore, when we see a now-uncommon Nassau grouper, it is no longer just another Nassau. It is an event.

—Cynthia Shaw

"You want me to turn a bit more to the left? Hokay."

About the Author and Illustrator

The daughter of a U.S. Naval officer, Cynthia Shaw grew up in Florida and the Caribbean, and later Missouri. She received a B.A. in zoology from the University of Hawaii-Manoa in 1980, with training in scientific illustration. An avid scuba diver and underwater photographer for over 25 years, Cynthia became involved in marine science and outdoor education when her first son started school in 1983. She has developed and taught ancillary science educational programs ever since. Also maintaining a freelance scientific illustration practice for many years, her illustrations have appeared in numerous scientific publications and museums. She currently develops supplementary science educational materials, and gives teacher workshops on incorporating scientific illustration in science classrooms. Cynthia resides in Washington State with her husband and three sons.